JACIN

To save her father from rotting in a
Mexican jail, Laurel had been forced
to marry the masterful Diego Ramirez,
a man she did not know and certainly
did not love—how could she, when she
was happily engaged to Brent? And
then Diego made it clear that the
marriage was *not* going to be in name
only . . .

JACINTHA POINT

BY
ELIZABETH GRAHAM

MILLS & BOON LIMITED
LONDON W1

First published 1980
Australian copyright 1980
Philippine copyright 1980
This edition 1980

© Elizabeth Graham 1980

ISBN 0 263 73283 5

Set in Linotype Baskerville 10 on 11½ pt.

Made and printed in Great Britain by
Richard Clay (The Chaucer Press), Ltd., Bungay, Suffolk

CHAPTER ONE

'LADIES *and gentlemen—señores y señoras—*Madeleine Fashions welcomes you to this our first Acapulco showing. Taking our cue from the glorious warmth of sun and sea surrounding us, we are using "Elegance in the Sun" as our theme.

'Many of you will be wondering if, or why, elegance is necessary in beach wear. We at Madeleine believe that elegance is every woman's prerogative, whether at the beach or in a sophisticated spot where she dances the night away.'

Laurel Trent's eyes, an unusual shade of green, swept round the audience seated at individual tables on either side of the long apron upon which the models would soon be displaying Madeleine creations. Most were American tourists—a sprinkling of younger groups there because a fashion show provided a contrast to the usual daytime amenities; the rest middle-aged men who mopped receding brows despite the air-conditioning, their wives obviously relishing the chance to sit down out of the sun and wiggle their toes in expensive sandals.

One couple caught and held her gaze, mostly because of the man's dark-eyed stare in her direction. No American this, with his high-bridged nose and stormy mouth, smoothly contoured jaw covered with the olive skin of his ancestors. The woman beside him was young and with a matching darkness of hair and eyes, her rounded figure lent drama by the black fully-sleeved dress she wore.

Laurel's gaze shifted back to the man and, finding his stare still as boldly penetrating, she pulled her eyes sharply back to the typed sheets before her.

'Mariella is going to begin today's showing in a sun and surf eyecatcher swimsuit and beach cover-up. . . .'

As the willowy dark girl, as slender as herself, walked on to the small stage, her nervous inexperience was apparent only to Laurel's practised eye. With a little more experience of this kind, the young Mexican girl would make an effective model. Laurel talked constantly in a soothingly confident tone as the girl paraded along the apron, using her hands to draw attention to the salient points of fit and design as Laurel mentioned them. The only real drop in Mariella's composure came as she neared the spot where the bold-eyed Mexican and his wife sat.

Puzzled as the girl retraced her steps tremblingly along the carpeted strip, Laurel glanced at the dark couple and saw that the man's brows were drawn down in an expression of severe disapproval. Obviously he hadn't taken kindly to the sight of one of his countrywomen exposing so much of her body to the interested gaze of the male spectators. With a faint shrug of dismissal at his Latin prejudice, Laurel went back to compering the show, proud on the whole that her teaching over the past weeks had not been in vain. As soon as the Mexican staff could handle things on their own, she would return to Los Angeles—and Brent.

But thoughts of her fiancé had to be put in abeyance while the show went on and finally reached its conclusion. Many of the American women in the audience, beguiled by the fashions that had looked so well on the slim models, were eagerly enquiring about placing orders. Elena, the girl who would be taking over as manager of the branch when Laurel returned to the States, directed them to the boutique located in the same hotel as that in which the fashion show had been held.

Backstage, Laurel warmly congratulated the four models on their maiden effort. All except Mariella smiled a shy acknowledgment, then drifted away to the dressing area.

'Is something wrong, Mariella?' Laurel adopted a casual stance against the utility table by the wall, crossing her arms over the waist of her sleeveless dress. The black background, overlaid by white-patterned scrolls, contrasted attractively with the silver-gilt of her hair, which was drawn back from her face in a smoothly sophisticated style. 'You were doing fine until you got down to the far end of the strip. What bothered you there?'

The dark girl hesitated, her eyes clouded. 'It was— Señor Ramirez. He does not like to see a woman dressed so, except perhaps on the beach.'

'Then he shouldn't come to a fashion show of beach wear!' Laurel responded tartly, then wrinkled her brow at the other girl. 'Who is he anyway, this Señor —Ramirez? Is he a relative of yours?'

'No—oh, no!' Mariella stared at her, horrified. 'He is Señor Diego Ramirez, one of the most important men in Mexico. Always his family has been powerful in the affairs of our country. Señor Diego is——'

'That doesn't give him the right to dictate where or when a woman can wear a swimsuit,' Laurel interrupted crisply, irritated anew that women living in the last

half of the twentieth century still obeyed the autocratic
rules and traditions of a bygone age. 'The lady with
him might have to accept his orders, but you certainly
don't.' She had noticed that several times, when the
dark girl by his side had turned to him excitedly about
one of the modelled swimsuits or figure-clinging
dresses, he had shaken his head impatiently.

'Ah, the poor Señora Ramirez,' Mariella mourned,
her brown eyes sympathetic. 'She has had much un-
happiness, although she is so young.'

'That I can believe,' Laurel returned with heartfelt
certainty, remembering the effect those dark appraising
eyes had forced on her. Señor Ramirez was evidently
one of those Latins who had one set of rules for women,
particularly his wife, and another completely opposite
code for his own behaviour.

Mariella scuttled away when the hotel's assistant
manager came to ask Laurel if the staff could begin to
clear the ballroom for that evening's buffet dance.
Giving her assent, Laurel cursorily checked the rack of
dresses and swim wear used for the afternoon show,
then made her way across the spacious yet intimate
ballroom to the wide glass doors giving on to the hotel's
huge lobby.

Live trees and shrubs in massive tubs were arranged
in seemingly haphazard manner across the immense
hall, and it was from behind one of these that the man
who had caused Mariella's fright stepped.

'Señorita Trent, may I speak with you for a moment?'

There was scarcely a trace of accent to his English—
a tribute to the expensive education he had no doubt
received in the best of American or European schools,
Laurel thought sourly. Beside the casually dressed

tourists, his off-white tropical suit and sober tie set a note of formal elegance. He was even taller than his seated position had indicated, and despite her own five foot six she had to tilt her head to look into the frank admiration in his dark eyes. From a distance they had appeared to be wholly black, but now she saw that they were a dark velvety brown and expressed precisely his emotions of the moment.

'I can't think of one thing we could possibly have in common to talk about, Señor Ramirez,' she said coolly, 'unless you have in mind an apology for scaring one of my young models out of her mind this afternoon.'

'Such was not my intention, Miss Trent,' he returned blandly, giving no inkling of whether he referred to an apology or to the fact of his unnerving Mariella.

'Then if you'll excuse me, Señor Ramirez,' Laurel attempted to sidestep him, but found her arm enfolded by a supple olive-skinned hand.

'You have learned my identity, Miss Trent,' he smiled, displaying a flash of white teeth and a deep ridge that ran down from cheek to mouth and did nothing to detract from his aristocratic good looks. 'Surely that is a hopeful sign for my intentions.'

'That depends on what your intentions are,' she snapped, drawing her arm away in irritation from the warm touch of his hand on her bare flesh. 'If my guess is correct, no proposition you have to make could possibly interest me.'

'You regard an invitation to dinner as a—proposition?'

'Dinner?' She stared at him blankly.

'Even a goddess of light and beauty must eat sometime,' he mocked softly. 'Can it be wrong for her to enjoy company while she does so?'

'You insult me, *señor*!'

Bewilderment that seemed genuine clouded his eyes. 'Insult? I do not understand. Why should a beautiful woman feel insulted because a man asks her to dine with him?'

As she swept away, Laurel tossed frigidly over her shoulder: 'Why don't you ask Señora Ramirez?'

There was a slight sense of satisfaction in the fleeting glimpse she caught of his quick frown, but anger pumped adrenalin through her veins as she walked quickly in the direction of the boutique.

How dared he exercise with her his male Latin assumption that, despite his married state, any woman was fair game for his pursuit! No wonder Mariella had described his wife as 'the poor Señora Ramirez' in that doleful way!

Her opinion remained unchanged the next day, which was the second and last showing, when Diego Ramirez appeared—alone. Mariella had failed to put in an appearance owing, she reported, to a stomach ailment. A sceptical Laurel, being closest in size to the absent Mariella, was forced to relinquish the microphone to Elena while she herself modelled the swimwear in place of the Mexican girl.

The first outfit, consisting of a black lacy cover jacket and provocatively revealing swimsuit, drew admiring glances from the audience, particularly from the perspiring American males accompanying their wives. Her long slender figure and silvery fair hair seemed made to mould the contours of the suit, and she was well used to the lascivious stares of the male element in an audience. What threw her on this occasion was the fury in Diego Ramirez's burning eyes. It was almost, she thought haughtily, swinging on her heel before his incensed eyes, as if her person belonged to him.

'It is unusual for a man like Señor Ramirez to attend a showing of fashions without the *señora*,' Elena remarked with an arch glance in Laurel's direction as they re-hung the garments on racks after the show. 'Perhaps he had some other *motivo* for coming, do you think?'

'Whatever his motive was, it doesn't concern me.' Laurel, feeling compunction because of her snappish reply, added to the crestfallen Elena: 'In my country, Elena, most men are not so obvious about their admiration for one woman while they are married to another.'

Elena's dark-toned face registered amazement. 'But Señor Ramirez is——'

'Excuse me, Señorita Trent,' the soft voice of the office clerk, Marta, interrupted. 'There is a telephone call for you, from Los Angeles.'

'Thank you, Marta, I'll come right away.'

Thoughts of Diego Ramirez were stripped from her mind as Laurel hurried across the hotel's sumptuous hall to the boutique. Tim Calder, the titular head of Madeleine Fashions in Los Angeles, no doubt wanted to know how the first showings of the house had gone in the Mexican Riviera resort of Acapulco. Her enthusiastic words of satisfaction with the business done died away in a gasp, however, when she recognised the male voice at the other end of the line.

'*Brent*! I thought it must be Tim calling to find out how things went with the shows.'

'Disappointed it's your fiancé instead?' he quipped, and she immediately conjured up a picture of his solid, fair good looks and attractively crooked smile.

'Of course not,' she returned breathlessly into the receiver. 'In fact, I—I wish you were here right now.'

'Sounds promising,' he chuckled, 'and I'd sure like
to follow it up, but this Melson case is brewing up to
something pretty big now.'

Brent was a rising young attorney, and the case he
referred to was a complicated one involving company
law, his speciality.

Laurel, who for some reason would rather have
heard foolishly romantic nothings from him, listened
patiently as he detailed that day's court appearance,
particularly his own. Why did her mind keep slipping
away from his pleasantly self-congratulatory voice to
dwell on a vision of a violently angry Mexican man
who looked capable of leaping up on the apron and
hustling her away to his thick walled castle in the
forest? As his *conquistador* ancestors would no doubt
have done. If it were he on the phone now, would he
be telling her the dull details of his day?—or would he
be whispering huskily of his longing for her?

'Wh-what did you say?' Realising suddenly that
Brent had asked a question and left silence on the line
for her answer, Laurel cleared her throat.

'I don't believe you've listened to a word I've said,'
he accused, sounding vaguely hurt and positively
angry.

'Of course I have. It's just—well, I've had a couple
of heavy days myself, and—maybe the heat's getting
to me.'

'It's been raining here for three days,' Brent sent
back starkly, 'so don't knock the sun!'

Laurel stared dully at the new filing cabinet beyond
the desk. No enquiry about her busy days, how the
shows had gone. Just—'don't knock the sun.'

'Laurel? Are you okay?'

'I'm fine,' she sighed.

'You're not falling for some Latin Romeo down there, are you? I've heard women can't resist them.'

Stung by his obvious amusement at that possibility, she retorted: 'As a matter of fact, there is one. He's very rich, influential, and he asked me to have dinner with him last night.'

'And did you?'

At last a note of personal interest! 'No, I'm engaged to you, remember?'

'Don't you forget it!'

'I'm not likely to, but—when, Brent? We don't have to wait. I can work for a while after we're married, so——'

'My wife is going to stay right at home and take care of me and the kids, in that order,' he said firmly. 'But we can't talk about this over the phone, for Pete's sake! And that reminds me, this call's costing an arm and a leg. I just wanted to call and explain why I haven't written lately. I'm even working nights on this case. How long will it be before you can leave things there?'

'I don't know yet.'

'Keep me posted.' His voice dropped a notch. 'I miss you, sweetie.'

'Yes. 'Bye, Brent.'

For a long time after replacing the receiver, Laurel sat pensively at the desk. Then with a long-drawn sigh she rose and made her way through the deserted salon, locking up as she went.

The small but efficient apartment leased for her for the duration of her stay in Acapulco was situated on the fourth floor of the Panorama Hotel where Madeleine Fashions was located.

Overlooking the tranquil vista of Acapulco Bay, with its sudden transitions from jewel toned sea to the velvet darkness of night, the apartment had been a constant source of interest and joy to Laurel. From her balcony she had watched para-sailors take off from the fine gold sand beach to soar over the blue-green waters of the Bay, all of the resort city at their feet. At night there was the booming resonance of the nearby Aztec Flyers' Show where, to the accompaniment of deeply rhythmic Mexican music smooth-muscled men gyrated in ever-increasing circles round a staunch centre pole reaching high into the night sky. From the volume of their applause, the tourists loved this attraction.

Tonight, however, when the blood-quickening music began for the first show, Laurel restlessly snapped the glass balcony doors shut. The harsh notes of trumpets, evocative of the primitive aspects of this vast and alien land, tonight made her feel uncomfortable. Strangely, the brash notes conjured up a sense of isolation, melancholy ... and a mental vision of Diego Ramirez. Though why the supremely self-assured Mexican should enter her mind for those reasons was completely beyond her. No man of her acquaintance had ever displayed more confident certainty of his supremacy in the scheme of things.

Deciding, after a cursory look into the interior of the apartment's refrigerator, to eat in the hotel's restaurant, Laurel showered quickly and dressed as hastily in a long dress of green floral cotton. The honey-gold tan she had acquired at the hotel's pool and sun-streaked beach was a perfect foil for the cool off-the-shoulder dress. Make-up was minimal—a touch of green eyeshadow to highlight her eyes, a smear of coral lipstick to outline a mouth made vulnerable by the fullness of its lower lip, a dusting of powder to give a matt appearance to small straight nose and unfreckled brow.

In the hall below, tourist men of differing nationality and states of sobriety blocked her path to the restaurant. 'Well, hi, honey!' was freely interspersed with what amounted to wolf calls in several languages, and Laurel wasn't sure if she was glad or sorry when a firm male hand clasped her elbow and an unequivocably Latin voice murmured:

'I have been waiting for you. Shall we dine here, or would you prefer somewhere more—intimate?'

Laurel gazed bemusedly at Diego Ramirez's expressive eyes, at present looking for all the world as if he had, indeed, been waiting for her to appear. His fingers, warm and vibrant, were still encircling her elbow, although he had removed her safely from the circle of her would-be admirers.

'There's no need for you to bother, Señor Ramirez,' she said stiffly, disengaging her arm. 'I can take care of myself.'

Dark brown eyes surveyed her smoothly tanned face. 'Perhaps. You are meeting someone?'

'No, I——' Laurel's lashes swept down, then lifted over eyes that met his boldly. 'I was on my way to eat at the hotel restaurant. They're used to seeing me on my own there.'

'Then permit me to escort you to the restaurant.' With an inclination of the head, he offered his arm and after a moment's hesitation she took it. Under other circumstances, his courtly gesture would have been mirth-provoking, but now Laurel felt a sense of reassurance when her fingertips rested on muscles as smoothly taut as a cougar's.

'Ah, Señorita Trent,' the *maitre d'hotel* greeted her, all smiles until his face registered shock at sight of her companion. 'Señor Ramirez!'

'*Como esta usted,* Tomas?'

'*Muy bien, gracias*! I will find a good table for you and Señorita Trent.' The beaming dining room chief was already turning away when Diego's regretful decline came.

'Unfortunately, I am not able to dine with Miss Trent tonight.' Turning the force of his dark eyes on her, he added in explanation: 'An unavoidable previous engagement.'

His tone suggested heartfelt regret, but Laurel, despite an illogical stab of disappointment, managed a cool: 'It's not important at all, Señor Ramirez. I had planned to eat alone.'

A light flickered behind his eyes, but he made no reply, turning instead to Tomas with a spate of Spanish too rapid for Laurel to follow. The words she did catch seemed to relate to 'Señora Ramirez' and a birthday celebration in her honour.

To her dismay, Tomas informed her after seating her in solitary splendour at a table for four overlooking the light-studded Bay that the celebration was to take place right here in the hotel dining room.

'My usual table would have been fine,' she told the suddenly solicitous Tomas. Normally, she had been escorted to a small table for two lining the wall and without a view.

'Señor Ramirez insists that in future you will have this table,' Tomas returned imperturbably, his eyes frankly curious as they went over her smoothly arranged silvery hair, the unusual colour of her eyes. 'He will be dining with you many times, *si*?'

'No,' Laurel returned firmly, glancing about her. '*El menu, por favor.*'

Rage seethed under her calm exterior as the chastened Tomas hastened across the room to speak with the table waiter. From his gestures and rolling eyes, she could well conjure up the words he spoke.

'The *señorita* at Table Fourteen is Señor Ramirez's latest girl-friend. See that she has everything she wants.'

If it hadn't been for the fact that it would be construed as an unwillingness to see him with his wife at the birthday celebration, Laurel would have forgone her dinner and returned to her room. As it was, she ordered the most simple meal on the menu from an obsequious waiter, who also brought a half bottle of expensive imported wine.

'I didn't order this,' she said crisply, sighing in exasperation when she heard the expected reply.

'Señor Ramirez has ordered it for you. It is the very best white wine we have, *señorita.*'

'Maybe so, but I don't want it. Take it away, please.'

Later, as she toyed with a sherbert dessert, she half regretted her high-handed refusal of the wine. The Ramirez celebration party, composed of several of what were evidently prominent Mexican socialites, occupied a long centre table with Diego Ramirez at one end, his wife at the other. The young woman was stunning in a lacy dress of all white scalloped cotton, the petulant droop of her mouth now lifted in happiness at the attention showered on her.

When Diego raised his glass of sparkling champagne, his eyes beaming a protective tenderness down the length of the table, Laurel rose hastily and made a swift retreat from the restaurant.

How could a man, so obviously devoted to his wife, make advances to another woman as if he were free to do so? Only a Latin ... a man who had a rigid set of rules for his wife to follow, but none for himself in amatory affairs.

CHAPTER TWO

A WEEK went by—a week during which Laurel exchanged not a word with Diego Ramirez, yet she was conscious of him in the background of her daily existence.

Several times during that week she had looked up from the customer she was dealing with to see his lithe form silhouetted against the glass of the display windows. When she visited the large market in search of her modest food requirements, he would be there, a stall or two away. Even in the echoing resonance of the church where she sought the spiritual calm that had been hers during all the years of her education in a Los Angeles convent, he was there at the far side of a back pew.

It was unnerving—but devastatingly successful if his purpose was to keep himself in her awareness. She found herself watching for him, knowing he would turn up somewhere in the line of her vision. And in an odd way, she knew that if she failed to feel his presence during any of her excursions outdoors she would know a ridiculous sense of anxiety.

Anxiety about what? she mocked herself as she lay on the hot sand behind the hotel the following Saturday afternoon. About the waning interest of a man locked into an indissoluble marriage in the Latin tradition? Even without considering Brent, her own husband-to-be, every facet of her early upbringing and religious education cried out against an illicit relationship with any man, however attractive he might be.

And Diego Ramirez was undoubtedly attractive, with a purely sensual appeal to a woman's susceptibilities. Something about him sent primitive senses clamouring for a satisfaction Laurel herself could only guess at.

She watched idly a scene unfolding further along the beach—a scene she had observed repeatedly during the weeks of her stay in Acapulco, and one which still had the power to sicken her. A young Mexican in swimming briefs, his body moulded like an Aztec warrior, had attracted the attention of a middle-aged American woman . . . one of the many who came, idle and rich, to seek a diversion denied them in their own respectable home community.

Leaning back on her beach towel, Laurel closed her eyes against the fierce heat of a sun that threatened to melt her body to a grease spot. Soon she would take a dip in the ocean, unafraid of the advances of beach boys. She was neither rich nor middle-aged, and they seemed to have an uncanny perception as to where their talents could be best employed.

Would Diego Ramirez have had to resort to being a beach boy lover of deprived women if his background had been the same as the young men she saw flirting along the beach? He'd have been excellent at it, she decided with a startling turn of thought. He must have been devastating as a young man, even without the confident air of sophistication he had acquired in the years since then.

Partly in rebellion against her thoughts, but mostly because of a cooling shadow cast across her face, Laurel blinked her eyes to openness and stared bemusedly up into Diego Ramirez's smouldering dark eyes. For the space of several drawn-out moments, each was aware of the other in a way which strangely excluded the other. A wholly male gaze took in the curving length of her female body, and Laurel's eye seemed compelled towards the supple smoothness of muscled flesh exposed in white swimming briefs.

'What are you doing here?' she gasped, wishing she could whip her beach towel around her, an impossibility because she was lying on it.

'I am here for the same reason as you, presumably—to swim.' He straightened away from her, his height impressive.

'Don't tell me you haven't your own private beach,' she said sarcastically, rising to a sitting position and hugging her knees with her arms.

Diego dropped down beside her. 'No beach is private in Mexico,' he commented drily, then gave her a sidelong look. 'However, I have a villa a few miles south, and tourists rarely venture that far from the attractions of Acapulco.'

'How nice to have enough money to buy privacy,' she jeered, dropping one hand to filter the fine sand through her fingers. With the other, she took sunglasses from her beach bag and slid them on to her nose.

'It is nice to have money,' he conceded. 'It also brings with it—responsibilities.'

His pause before the last word brought her obscured eyes round to observe him curiously. Somehow 'responsibilities' brought to mind the wife whose birthday he had celebrated so tenderly a few nights before.

'Do you have children?' she asked abruptly, and saw the swift narrowing of his eyes.

'None, I regret to say. But that is something for the future when the right—moment comes.'

Laurel smiled acidly and looked out to where the heads of swimmers bobbed on the green hued water. 'I thought that was the primary purpose when Latin men marry, to prove their *machismo* by forcing a child a year on their wives.'

Good grief, what a conversation to be having with a man she scarcely knew, let alone one who had Spanish nobility stamped on every feature of his stormy face!

'Force should not be necessary in such matters,' he decreed softly, bringing a touch of rose to her skin with a penetrating stare that pierced the smoked glass covering her eyes. 'You have no man?'

'What?'

'It is strange for a beautiful woman to be lying on a beach alone, with no man to protect her from others who lust for her with their eyes.' His supple brown hand indicated with a wave the assorted unattached men who had, indeed, been sending hopeful glances her way since her arrival on the beach. Not the beach boys, but Americans for the most part who were obviously determined to make the most of their two-week vacation in what they had heard was swinging Acapulco. And maybe it was for them.

'I can take care of myself,' she snapped, suddenly remembering the lacy overtop she had brought. Reaching behind her, she slid her arms into the loose sleeves and hugged the scanty garment round her. 'To answer your question, yes, I do have a man. My fiancé is in Los Angeles.'

There was a sharp hiss of indrawn breath, but she kept her eyes averted from the smooth features. Really, the colossal nerve of men—and she had encountered many in her career—who blithely ignored their own

wives sitting at home, but showed resentment at her
own loyalty to Brent!

'You are engaged to be married, yet you do not wear
his ring?' he asked caustically after a while.

'I have his ring. I—I didn't want it to get lost in
the sand, that's all.'

'And you are also afraid to lose it where you work?'

Laurel flashed him an irritated look. 'My employers
prefer that I wear no jewellery apart from what they
supply with the fashions. And now, if you'll excuse me,
señor,' she rose with her habitual grace and collected
up her things, 'I'll leave you to enjoy the swim you
came for.'

'I can swim at any time,' he shrugged carelessly, and
to her chagrin he walked back across the sand to the
hotel with her. But even as rage prickled at her skin
like heat rash, she noticed that women of all ages took
a second look at his superb masculine figure, and
spared a third for a glance at herself.

He held open the glass door for her to pass into the
delightful coolness of the air-conditioned lobby, and at
the bank of elevators opposite the long reception counter he leaned nonchalantly against the wall, towel
draped round his neck, while Laurel waited impatiently for a vacant elevator.

'Will you have dinner with me tonight?' he asked
with an imperious lift of one black brow. 'It is not
right for a woman to eat alone in a place such as this.'
His eyes went with lazy eloquence round the sumptuously furnished lobby.

'I prefer to eat alone rather than dine in the company of a well-known man who happens to be married.'
She waved a slim hand in the direction of the glass
doors leading to the beach. 'Why do you waste your

time on me? There must be dozens of women out there who'd jump at the chance and ask no questions.'

'*Si*,' he sighed, one corner of his mouth quirking in a half smile. 'But it is in my nature to play the part of the hunter, not the prey.'

The words sent a chill down Laurel's spine, and she shivered despite herself. It would be easy to picture such a man relentlessly stalking his prey until in sheer exhaustion it gave up.

'Fine,' she summoned crisply. 'Just as long as you do your hunting in another neck of the woods from mine.'

'I think not,' he said softly, his eyes following her into the elevator which had at last arrived. '*Hasta la vista*, Laurel.'

For almost a week it was as if Diego Ramirez had disappeared from the face of the earth—or at least from the Acapulco scene. And although Laurel told herself that she felt only relief that his pursuit had ceased, illogically she missed his unmistakable presence in the background of her existence.

But when she was called to the shop's telephone the following Friday afternoon and heard his distinctive accent, irritation lent a ragged edge to her voice.

'Will you please stop pestering me?' she gritted through her teeth, glaring so hard at the intrigued Marta that the girl scurried out of the small office. 'If you don't, Señor Ramirez, I'll find someone who will stop you!'

The threat of officialdom left him unperturbed, and there was even a husky laugh in his voice when he returned: 'Such a fiery temper for so cool a beauty! But my intention is not to pester, Laurel, simply to ask you to have dinner with me tonight.'

'That comes under the label of pestering, *señor*!' she snapped. 'How many times do I have to tell you that I'm not interested?'

'You would be doing me a great favour, Laurel,' he went on persuasively, ignoring her question. 'I have to entertain a business associate, a countryman of yours and his wife, and it would be better if the numbers were even.'

It was as if the lines were crossed and they were having different conversations. 'It's impossible, *señor*.'

'You have an engagement for tonight?' he asked sharply.

The word 'engagement' reminded her of Brent, and she said sweetly: 'Yes, I have. With my fiancé.'

His swiftly indrawn breath hissed in her ear, and after a fractional silence he said stiffly: 'I see. Then of course I must find another partner.'

'As I've said before, that shouldn't be too much of a problem for you,' she told him acidly, then dropped the receiver back in its cradle.

For a few further moments she stood thoughtfully over it, biting irritably on her soft lower lip. Now the dratted man had forced her to tell an untruth, and she was uncomfortable with dishonesty. Mingled with that was a nagging reminder that she would be spending the evening alone, as usual. Her imagination leapt to the evening she might have had in Diego Ramirez's company, sensing instinctively that he would be any woman's dream of an escort, witty, suave, handsome. And too well aware of it for her liking!

She was back in her apartment pondering her plans for dinner when she remembered the way her name sounded on his lips. His emphasis on the 'r' in the middle gave it a special quality it had never had for her before, a senuously caressing sound. She hadn't told him her name, or that he could use it, but it would have been a simple thing for him to have found out.

The phone rang noisily on its table beside the colourfully upholstered couch, and she went quickly to answer it, the thought half formulated that perhaps Diego had found out somehow that Brent wasn't in town after all. Then all thoughts of both men flew from her mind when she heard the voice at the other end of the line.

'Dad! Is it really you? Where are you?'

The questions tumbled from Laurel's lips, and her father gave his unmistakable chuckle.

'Hold on there, honey! I'm right here in Acapulco. A couple of fellows chartered my boat in L.A., so I thought it would be a great chance to visit my one and only daughter.'

'How long are you going to be here?'

'Just a few days. These fellows were hell bent on getting to Mexico City—though it would have been a lot quicker to have hopped on a plane. But they said they wanted to fish on the way down and back, though neither of them seemed to know one end of a rod from the other.'

In her joy at hearing her one remaining parent's voice, Laurel dismissed the two faceless men. 'That's not important. What I want to know is, when can I see you?'

'Well, I have to pick up a couple of things for the boat, so how would it be if I come right along to the hotel after that? Let's really celebrate, baby, and have dinner somewhere special. You must know all the best places by now,' he teased.

'We could go to the El Mirador and you can see the

divers go off the cliff after dark,' Laurel responded elatedly. 'It's quite a sight.'

'Whatever you think, honey. Can you make reservations from there?'

Assuring him that she would, Laurel hung up the receiver and lifted it again almost immediately to dial the hotel. She made the reservation for eight-thirty. That would give them time to eat a leisurely dinner before watching the spectacular display from the lounge overlooking the cliffs.

She took a hurried shower, then selected one of the dresses supplied by Madeleine Fashions to advertise their wares even in her off-duty hours. It was a black figure-hugging creation which contrasted sharply with the silvery sheen of her hair. Her mind was filled with thoughts of her father while she sat at the mirrored dressing table and swept her hair into a sophisticated chignon style.

Since her mother's death, Dan Trent seemed to have given up on all the aspects of his life that had been meaningful until then. The brokerage business in which he had made great strides despite his youth, the home he had shared with his wife ... even, Laurel had sometimes thought, on the daughter their love had produced. Two months after her mother's death, she had been consigned to the care of the convent, and her father had bought a cabin cruiser which, when money supplies ran low, he chartered out with himself as skipper.

Vacations for the young Laurel were occasions when she could escape the sometimes stifling atmosphere of the convent and share the nomadic life of her father aboard *Dainty*—he had christened the boat with the pet name he had had for his petite wife.

Tears threatened to destroy her carefully applied mascara as her father's familiar sequence of knocks sounded on the outer door. How often had she heard those special taps when, as a teenager, he had sought to rouse her from her adolescent lethargy aboard *Dainty*?

'Dad—oh, Daddy, it's so good to see you!'

There was a blur of laughing blue eyes set in a ruggedly handsome sea-tanned face before Laurel was engulfed in a hearty embrace from which she extricated herself moments later, laughing and blinking away tears.

It wasn't until later, when they sat opposite each other at an elegantly laid table, that Laurel took time to study her father's face in any detail. What she saw there sent a tiny stab of apprehension through her. Surely there were stress marks more deeply etched round his eyes, more deeply embedded round his generous mouth? But the reddish brown of his thick hair remarkably held just a sprinkling of grey, and as Laurel noticed the speculative glances in his direction by several women dining in their vicinity, she marvelled anew that he had never married again.

She had been aware of women on the periphery of his life, but none of them had tempted him from his widower status. Memory conjured up visions of darkly voluptuous women, the occasional redhead or brunette. But none had resembled her Dresden-fair mother, whose silvery beauty she herself had inherited.

Now Dan Trent's inimitable chuckle drew her attention back to him.

'Don't look round now, honey, but there's a man sitting over there in a party of four who's looking at me as if he'd like to revive the Spanish Inquisition! Looks as if his ancestors had a big part in that, too!

You been playing fast and loose with Spanish gran-
dees?'

Without looking round, Laurel knew that he must
be referring to Diego Ramirez. Drat the man! Why
did he have to turn up wherever she went, particularly
now when she was with her father after telling him
that it was Brent she would be with.

'No,' she answered drily. 'He's like a lot of Latins—
wants to play fast and loose with me, while keeping
his respectable wife safely in the background!'

'He's married?' Dan ejaculated, startled eyes sweeping over to the table behind Laurel's shoulder. 'To
that beautiful dark woman with him? Then why in
hell is he looking at me as if I'm stealing cookies from
his jar?'

Laurel shrugged. 'Pay no attention. Spanish men
have one rule for themselves and another for women.'

To her dismay, her father turned belligerent. 'If he
thinks he's going to treat my daughter like some floozie
in a——'

'I can take care of myself, Dad!' she told him sharply.
Her eyes strayed involuntarily to the ring on her third
finger. 'I'm engaged to Brent, remember?'

'I remember,' he rejoined soberly, his eyes joining
hers in contemplation of the subdued sparkle of taste-
ful diamonds flanked by two small rubies.

That her father cared little for Brent had been obvious almost from their first meeting. True, Brent's
innate sense of propriety had looked askance at Dan
Trent's nomadic way of life the first time Laurel had
taken him to the marina where *Dainty* was berthed,
and his attitude had made a permanent impression on
her father. But he had nonetheless respected his daughter's choice of a man to share her life with.

'I'm going to powder my nose, Dad,' she said impulsively, leaning across the table to lay a light hand on his forearm, 'then we'll go find a good spot to watch the divers, hm?'

'Okay with me, honey,' he smiled warmly up at her as she passed on her way to the powder room, making her conscious again of how attractive he was. She wished fleetingly as she wended her way between the tables that he had found a woman who could at least partially replace her mother. He deserved more than the lonely life he led most of the time.

In the powder room she renewed her lipstick and powdered the beginning shine on her nose, then, with a last cursory glance at her all-over appearance, she stepped out into the foyer. Intent on securing the clasp on her black fabric evening purse, she missed seeing the dark-clad figure which appeared from behind a spreading potted shrub until she cannoned painfully against its steely contours. Pivoting back on her heels, she looked up into an implacably cold male face.

'You!' she gasped, then shook her head in wonderment. 'Why are you always popping out from behind trees and things?'

'I have been waiting here to talk to you,' Diego Ramirez said furiously, his jaw twitching angrily.

'So? Talk.' Laurel mustered all her coolness to look squarely into the flashing eyes. 'My—companion is waiting for me.'

'That is exactly what I wish to talk to you about,' he said heatedly, ignoring the curious looks of passers-by. 'He is too old for you!'

'Who's too old?' she stared at him, bewildered, and then enlightenment came. 'You mean——?'

'I mean your fiancé,' he answered roughly. 'He is old

enough to be your father!'

Laurel suppressed the giggles threatening to spill
over into glorious laughter. He actually thought that
Dan was her fiancé! Hence the reason for his dark
looks in Dan's direction.

'But he's——' she began weakly, then cool logic took
over. Wasn't it all to the good that he should believe
Dan was Brent? Dan was solid, a tangible evidence of
her prior commitment. 'He's—much younger than his
years really, once you get to know him.'

'*Bah!*' Diego Ramirez said with Spanish contempt.
'His life has already been lived, yet you want to tie
yourself to such a man?' His eyes swept round the
foyer, noting the women passing in twos and threes
from the powder room. His hand shot out and grasped
her wrist, jerking her to him behind the potted shrub.
'What can he teach you of love, of passion?' he demanded furiously. 'Does he kiss you like this?'

Suddenly she was pulled against the steely hardness
of his body, her breasts crushed to the hard expanse of
his chest, her thighs yieldingly soft against his taut
muscles. His mouth descended without warning and
took possession of her shocked lips while his hands
arched her to the bend of his body. His kiss was like
nothing she had ever experienced before, and left her
breathless when his hold at last slackened.

'Let me go!' she choked, pushing with her fists
against his chest until he let her go so suddenly that
she swayed uncertainly.

'No,' his voice came as from a distance, 'he has not
kissed you with passion.'

'How long is it since you kissed your wife that way,
señor?' she blazed wildly at him, then broke away and
half ran across the foyer, arriving breathless at the

table where her father still sat.

'Oh, there you are, Laurel. Sit down and have some more coffee, honey. I hear we have lots of time.'

'Well, I——' she hesitated, then saw Diego Ramirez's commanding figure approaching their table. Feeling faint, she sank back into her chair and watched mesmerised as he came, paused to stare fractionally into the darkened green of her eyes, then pass on to his own table.

Her eyes met Dan's and dropped away in embarrassment. His bright blue gaze seemed to hold the knowledge of the scene that had taken place in the foyer, although there was no way he could have seen anything from the angle he was sitting at.

'Wasn't that your Spanish admirer?' he asked teasingly, yet something about his smile spoke of tiredness, a deep-down weariness he had been doing his best to hide.

'What? Oh. Yes.'

Dan looked at the tip of the fat cigar he had lit. 'I sure wish Brent would look at you with one quarter of the feeling that Mexican put into it a minute ago,' he said almost casually.

Laurel stared across at him speechlessly, then brought out: 'Brent—loves me, Dad. He wants me to be his wife. Isn't that enough?'

'Sure, baby,' he patted her arm gently. 'If it's enough for you, then I guess I have no say in it. But, Laurel,' he leaned towards her with unusual gravity, 'don't mistake security for love, passion, and—all the other things that go into making a perfect marriage. Brent's a nice guy, he'll never beat you or let you go without something he can provide for you. You'll have a good social life, with a nice home in the suburbs somewhere, and he'll give you two point five children or whatever the latest statistics dictate, but——' He paused heavily, then sighed. 'I'm not putting this very well, honey, but —hell, it's not what your mother and I had,' he ended fiercely.

'I know, Dad,' Laurel said unsteadily, her darkened lashes blinking away the tears that threatened to fall uninhibitedly. 'But I long ago came to the conclusion that what you and Mom had was something too rare and precious to come around too often in a human life span. 'So,' she smiled tremulously, 'I'll have to be content with someone who loves me and will take care of me—and the two point five kids!'

'Okay, honey. Let's go see these divers.'

Laurel was only too happy to scoop up her bag again and follow him from the dining room, though she couldn't resist a sideways glance towards the table where Diego Ramirez sat. The middle-aged couple looked like average Americans, and the woman looking up to follow Diego's gaze was breathtakingly lovely. A smile of contempt edged Laurel's lips. As she had suspected, it hadn't proved difficult for him to find an attractive partner for the evening. Her hand came up to her hair in an automatic smoothing gesture and she saw Diego's mouth tighten at the sight of her engagement ring.

Stepping quickly to catch up with Dan, she put her hand on his arm and felt the warmth of the smile he sent down into her strained expression.

There was no time for more than a few quick exchanges before their attention was diverted to where the cliff outside was illuminated in eerie brilliance. A young diver, bronzed skin gleaming, was poised on the rocks two thirds of the way up the jagged cliffside, his head bent contemplatively on the swirling water be-neath. Laurel, having witnessed the breathtaking div-ing spectacle several times, quickly explained the technical aspects of the dive to her father.

'They have to time it very carefully, watching for a wave that brings the diving depth to twelve feet—normally the water's only eight feet, so the extra depth makes quite a difference.'

'I guess so,' Dan returned drily, his eyes bright as they fastened on the diver. 'He must have to take quite a leap off the side to miss those rocks under him.'

'He does—look, he's going now!'

The diver had raised his arms, and there was a con-certed gasp as the lithe body leapt from the rock and dived, arms outstretched like a graceful bird plunging to gather sustenance from the sea. The arrowed body sliced into the green water, leaving very little spray, and the dark head and shoulders reappeared seconds later.

Laurel turned with a sigh to give her father one of her rare and quite beautiful smiles, aware suddenly that his hand was clasping hers tightly.

'That was really something, wasn't it?' he said, awed.

'Wait till you see the other divers go off the top,' Laurel laughed. 'I've seen it a few times, but it still gives me goosepimples.' She pointed to the cliff top. 'They go from there, and it's about a hundred and twenty feet up.'

'I don't know that my heart can stand that much excitement,' Dan smiled, a frown settling over his strongly marked brows as he took in the animated beauty of his daughter's face ... a face so like the wife's he had lost that he had found it difficult to be with Laurel on her vacations from the convent school.

'It'll have to,' she chuckled, her eyes sweeping round
the sea of faces pressing around them for the show.
'There's no way we can get out of——' Her voice died
away as her eyes met those of Diego Ramirez, his holding such a dark glitter of some deep emotion that the
remainder of the words froze in her throat.

Dan, puzzled by her sudden abstraction, glanced up
in the direction her eyes took, and his gaze went rapidly between his daughter and the man who seemed
to see nothing but Laurel. The vivid dark girl who
stood by his side had missed nothing of the encounter
either, judging by the snapping flash of her fine eyes.

'Laurel?' he said gently. 'Honey?'

'Wh-what?' Her lids blinked as if she were awaking
from a dream. 'Oh, look, Dad, the really high divers are
about ready to go.'

There was a thoughtful gleam in Dan's eyes as they
went to the outdoor scene, where a more mature diver
stood still as the rock he topped. He, too, watched intently the surge of green water into the chasm below,
timing his swallow dive to the rhythm of the incoming
flood.

As the graceful body cleaved through the waves,
Laurel released her pent-up breath in a sigh in unison
with the collective groan from the people around her.
What must it be like to dive like that into unknown
depths with precision timing? To leave the past behind, perhaps for ever.

Her bemused gaze lifted and met fractionally with
Diego Ramirez's steady-eyed intensity. It was as if those
eyes had been pinned on her all through the spectacular dive, and for a moment her scalp seemed to tighten
in some strange kind of recognition. Then she was
laughing with her father, rising to leave as spectators

for the next show pressed forward. Of the Ramirez party, there was suddenly no sign.

Back at her hotel apartment, Dan refused a nightcap.

'I'll take a raincheck, honey,' he said, smiling wearily, 'until tomorrow night. You'll have dinner with me on board?' At her acquiescent nod, he added ruefully: 'Can't offer you anything more appetising than hard tack at the moment, but——'

'I can take a hint,' Laurel smiled with pretended wryness. 'I'll pick up some things at the market tomorrow and make us a meal fit for the gods.'

Dan reached for the door handle. 'I'm not sure I come into that category, but it'll be nice pretending. About six?'

Laurel nodded, and reached up to kiss his cheek before closing the door behind him. As she prepared for bed, two faint lines worried her smooth brow.

An elusive something had intruded between her and her father that night. Nothing specific that she could put her finger on, but it had been there, lurking behind their lighthearted talk, all evening.

CHAPTER THREE

MEXICAN drivers had to be the worst—or maybe it was the best—drivers in the world, Laurel thought late the next afternoon as she manoeuvred her unpredictable rental car along the Costera Miguel Alemán, the broad avenue linking the network of high-rise beach hotels ringing the Bay. A Mexican businessman had told her at a party that the driver's sense of *machismo* was involved.

'It is a race for dominance in a male world, Señorita Trent,' he had explained with a wry smile. 'It makes no difference whether the prize is a woman, or a few yards gained on a highway. He must do all he can to assert his superiority.'

The words came back to haunt her as she tried vainly to change from one traffic lane to another which would take her to the yacht harbour. Then suddenly a gap was left for her by a taxi driver who pantomimed his appreciation of her fair beauty.

Disregarding the rolling eyes, Laurel slipped into the space and minutes later was pulling up into the yacht club's parking lot.

Bearing the makings of an American-type meal which she was sure her father would prefer, she walked along the pier and a lump came to her throat when she saw *Dainty* tied up towards the end. She might not be the sleekest, most modern vessel afloat, but some of Laurel's happiest memories were tied up in her sturdy frame.

There was no sign of Dan Trent as she stepped on
to the afterdeck, balancing the brown paper bag on her
hip.

'Dad?' she called, going to the steps leading down to
the compact galley and roomy saloon beyond it. 'I'm
here, Dad!'

Quiet still prevailed, so she ventured down the narrow steps and contemplated the meticulously neat
galley area. Whatever else Dan Trent might neglect
in his life, it was never the care and upkeep of his beloved boat.

The saloon, with its long centre table and gaily upholstered seating areas, was similarly unoccupied, but
Laurel stood for a while inhaling the dearly familiar
scents of the sea and her father's lingering cigar smoke.
Nostalgia closed her throat again, and tears threatened
the mascara she had applied lightly to her lashes. How
she would have loved to be a vagabond, a rover of the
seas, with her father.

But he had listened to the nuns, who had been concerned about her future. The thought of a motherless
girl roaming the world with a devil-may-care father
had brought tremors to their gentle souls.

So she had been brought up chastely, respectably, by
women who had renounced the worldly scene apart
from the young charges in their care. All expect her beloved Sister Carmelita, the sweet-faced nun who had
taught her not only Spanish, but a sense of her feminine
destiny.

'One day a man will come into your life, Laurel,' she
had said softly after Laurel had burst out that she,
too, would become a nun. 'A man who will fill your
life with his very presence, who will love and cherish
you and give you children to nourish and care for.

After all,' she had laughed gently, 'if Christ chose all women to be His brides, there would be no channel for new souls to be born into this world. No, Laurel, it is my feeling that He has other plans for you.'

The transitory desire had soon faded from Laurel's mind, as it had from most of her classmates who had had similar leanings. But Sister Carmelita's words had become etched into her subconscious so that, when Brent Halliday had come along, he seemed the answer to Laurel's questions about her future. He was wholesome, clean-cut, and willing to wait for the marriage ceremony before consummating their love ... a rarity in an age of sexual permissiveness.

Footsteps sounded on the deck above, and Laurel snapped out of her reverie and rushed to the foot of the steps.

'Dad? Where have you been? I hope you haven't been out buying things for dinner, because I——'

Abruptly she stopped, her widened gaze staring bewilderedly up into Diego Ramirez's eyes. Her peripheral vision noted that he looked as nautical as any sailor on the pier in dark blazer jacket and white slacks, a casually knotted silk scarf giving him a more elegant look than most.

Instantly she froze. 'What are you doing here?' she demanded coldly. 'I'm really getting quite sick and tired of you following me wherever I go, Señor Ramirez! My father will be here at any minute, so I'd advise you to leave right now.'

He made no immediate reply to her accusation, gesturing instead to the lower portion of the boat. 'May I come down?' he enquired politely, then, disregarding her vehement negative, his highly polished black shoes descended the narrow stairway and he stood before her, far too close for her comfort.

'My father,' she gritted through her teeth, 'will be back any minute now, and I warn you he won't be one bit pleased to see you here on his boat!'

Far from being cowed by the threat, Diego glanced round the saloon before indicating one of the broad couches with an olive-skinned hand.

'I think you should sit down, Laurel. I have something important to tell you.'

'Really! Well, you'd better make it snappy, whatever it is you have to say,' she told him imperiously, 'because I'm just about to start cooking dinner for my father and myself.'

The slight, regretful shake of his head irritated her beyond measure, yet sent an odd stab of apprehension along her nerve ends. But what could Diego Ramirez possibly have to tell her that would give her cause for alarm? In another moment she found out.

'I am afraid that your father will not be joining you for dinner tonight,' he informed her, his eyes intensely dark as they rested on the suddenly apprehensive green of hers.

'Not——?'

'No,' he said regretfully, then sighed. 'Your father has unfortunately been detained by the *policia*.'

'*Pol*——?' Laurel stared at him speechlessly, her heart beginning an unsteady thrum at his next words.

'I have a berth on this same pier,' he went on tonelessly, 'and noticed some agitation at this boat when I docked late this afternoon. I recognised the man who was being led away by police as the one who escorted you to El Mirador last night.' His eyes gleamed momentarily. 'The man I thought must be your fiancé.'

Ignoring the last part, Laurel jumped agitatedly to

her feet. 'But why would the police come for my father? He's never done anything illegal in his whole life! There must be some terrible mistake—I have to go to him, tell them ...'

Diego raised a detaining hand and rested it on her forearm. 'Later, perhaps. I was able to find out from the arresting officers that your father is involved in the smuggling of drugs. As you may know, this is a serious offence in Mexico.'

'Drug smuggling?' she repeated stupidly, her mind a sea of cotton suddenly. 'My father? That's crazy ... crazy!'

'Sit down, Laurel,' Diego commanded in such a way that her knees folded automatically. He remained standing himself, braced against the dark wood of the dining table. 'You must realise that this is a serious charge against your father. From the evidence found on this boat, he could be detained indefinitely—even before any trial takes place.'

Laurel's hands went up to cover her face, and her voice was a muffled thread when she said: 'Trial? Dad? I can't believe this is happening!'

'Even so, it is happening. I went to the police station and was able to talk with your father very briefly. He told me that the men who chartered his boat in Los Angeles returned early this morning, but left again almost immediately, saying they would return tonight and sail early tomorrow.'

'The men—that's it!' Laurel cried wildly, jumping to her feet again. 'Dad told me they'd hired the boat for a fishing trip, but they didn't know the first thing about fishing!' She made a dash for the companion-way. 'I have to tell the police——'

'Don't be ridiculous!' Diego snapped with such

force that her feet halted in their tracks. Coming to her, he grabbed her shoulders fiercely. 'Do you think they will listen to you, his daughter?'

'Don't you see, I have to do something?' Strangely, at that moment Laurel questioned not at all his right to interfere with her movements, with her wish to visit her father in a foreign prison. Her eyes clung in desperation to the penetrating darkness of his, and she saw there the quick change from impersonal solicitude to hardness of purpose.

'There is nothing you can do, Laurel—not, in any case,' he emphasised heavily, 'with the authorities.'

'Then where?' she cried desperately, no longer feeling the dry heat of his hands on her shoulders. 'Is there an American consul in Acapulco?'

'In Mexico City there is a consular office, but I can assure you that the consul's hands are tied in such matters.'

'But you seemed to think there's something I can do! Just tell me and I'll do it.'

For the space of a few moments he stared into the sea green of her eyes, then his lids dropped and he turned from her.

'I am not without power in certain circles,' he told her, his voice huskily subdued.

'Then you'll do something to help my father?' Laurel asked with sudden eagerness, taking a step towards him but flinching when he turned back to face her, his eyes intense black orbs raking her face.

'My influence would be much greater if——' His pregnant pause unaccountably sent her pulses racing, but she stared fixedly at him. 'If you were my wife, Laurel.'

*

Still Laurel stared at him, noting despite her shock the long curve of his black lashes, the faint shadow on his leanly moulded jaw, the male firmness of mouth which she suspected would compress into cruelty if occasion demanded.

'Wife?' The word was a mere whisper as her eyes clung to his. 'But you already have a wife.'

His shake of the head held a hint of impatience. 'No, I have never been married. The woman you think of as my wife is my younger brother's widow. Jaime was killed last year competing in a motor boat race.'

'But you let me think—I believed that——' Laurel broke off, her mind whirling with this added knowledge.

'Yes, I admit I let you think that Consuelo was my wife,' he conceded stiffly. 'That was not my intention in the beginning, but when you assumed that the woman with me at the fashion show was married to me, I wanted to find out how far you would resist the advances of a man you took to be married.' His expression softened somewhat. 'And you did reject me on those grounds.'

As far from enlightenment as ever, Laurel shook her head to clear it. Her mind was still experiencing shock waves from the news of her father's predicament, and Diego's words meant little to her.

'I still don't understand. Are you saying that you were *testing* me in some way?'

'In a manner of speaking, yes.' Diego half turned from her and took a cigar case from his pocket, his long olive-toned fingers extracting a thin cheroot and applying an expensive gold lighter to it. Feeling the trembling of her knees, Laurel sank back on the divan and stared numbly up at his smoothly formed body. 'It is very important to me that my wife should be above reproach in such matters.'

Something about the arrogantly proud lift of his head as he stood gazing from a porthole, the sun-kissed waters reflecting shimmering lights over his brown skin, started Laurel's reflexes into clearer motion.

'You must be *loco*,' she said in sudden wrath. 'Even if I wanted to marry you—which I don't!—you seem to forget that I have a fiancé, a man I'm going to marry on my return to Los Angeles.'

Diego slanted a narrowed look down at her indignantly flushed face. 'You are in love with this man?'

'Of course I am!' Laurel got to her feet and paced back towards the galley before turning to face him again, pinpoints of anger flashing in her eyes. 'Would I be marrying him if I wasn't?'

'Perhaps,' he shrugged, and flicked the narrow band of white ash from his cigar into the receptacle behind him. 'Women marry for different reasons—money, position, security, as well as for love. He is a wealthy man, this fiancé of yours?'

'No, he isn't,' Laurel snapped. 'He's a struggling young lawyer, so you can rule out the first two of your conditions.'

'So it must be the third, security,' he mused, leaning back to perch on one corner of the dining table. 'Is that what he offers you? A home in a "good" subdivision, thoughtfully spaced children, Saturday night at the country club?' His words held all the derision of a super-wealthy man for the masses, as well as revealing his knowledge about the American middle class way of life.

'What's wrong with those things?' she demanded, advancing a step or two to add sarcastically: 'Not everybody can afford a winter home in Acapulco and a no doubt palatial town house in Mexico City!'

Diego took a deep drag on his cigar. 'Nothing is wrong with those things,' he returned evenly, 'as long as the woman wants them for the right reason. Namely, that she loves passionately the man who provides them.'

'And that brings us to the fourth condition, which is——' Laurel stopped abruptly and pressed her fingers to her temples. 'Why are we talking about these non-sensical things when my father is rotting in one of your Mexican jails? You're making me as crazy as you are!'

'Not crazy—expedient.' Diego straightened fluidly from the table, stubbing out his cigar in the ashtray. 'I admit that our prisons leave a lot to be desired, particularly where drug cases are concerned, but your father has not yet started to rot, as you call it. I was able to arrange to have a meal brought to him and some other small comforts.'

'Thank you,' she choked bitterly. 'Money speaks, doesn't it?'

'In this case, not entirely.' When he paused fractionally, Laurel lifted her eyes searchingly to his. 'The officials were influenced more by my relationship to your father than in money.'

She stared blankly into the darkness of his eyes. 'Relationship? There is no relationship between——' Her eyes widened in disbelief. 'You told them that—that——'

'I told them that you were to become my wife,' he informed her crisply, his eyes meeting hers boldly, 'and that it would not be expedient for me to have my future father-in-law treated like a common criminal.'

'How dared you!' Laurel breathed, her skin paling to alabaster.

'You object to your father receiving good treatment?' he asked, one well-marked eyebrow lifting high on his brow.

'I object to you securing it for him under false pretences,' she flared angrily, clasping her hands and wringing them before her. 'Did you also lie to my father?'

'Lie? No. I told him of my wish to marry you, and that this could be accomplished sooner than expected because of the circumstances.' Diego moved forward and caught at her sleeveless arms, forcing her to look up into his sober expression. 'I had intended a more leisurely courtship, *querida*, but——'

'Don't call me that!' Laurel jerked away from his imprisoning hands. 'I'm not your darling, and never will be!'

'So.' Diego moved abruptly past her and paused with one foot on the bottom step of the companionway. His eyes held a fiery contempt as he turned his head to look at her. 'If you should change your mind, *señorita*, you may telephone to Jacintha Point, my villa.' Taking a small pad from his pocket, he scribbled some figures on it before tearing off the sheet and handing it to her. 'This is an unlisted number, so don't lose it. *Adios*.'

Laurel's nerveless fingers clutched the scrap of paper as her eyes dully watched his white slacks and polished shoes disappear to the upper deck. Then, feeling suddenly bereft, she turned back into the saloon, dropping the paper on the table before subsiding once more into the cushioned upholstery.

The clearly defined telephone number seemed to

leap from the table and become immediately engraved on her heart. But there must be some way, some means, of having her father released without Diego Ramirez's solution of her marriage to a powerful Mexican national.

'May I help you, *señorita*?'

Used as she was to male admiration while she demonstrated Madeleine Creations, Laurel flinched under the lascivious stare of the unranked policeman who lounged outside the station, a cigarette dangling from his lips.

'I—I want to see my father, Daniel Trent.'

'You are *norte-americana*?' he asked inquisitively, his eyes dropping appreciatively to the pencil-slim dress in pale green which Laurel had hurriedly changed into at the hotel. The outline of her figure was clearly visible under the brief white shawl covering her shoulders, and she pulled it closer round her neck.

'Just tell me where I can find the officer in charge,' she commanded frostily.

'*Si, señorita*, but maybe he is busy for a while, eh?'

His lewd expression spoke volumes as to how he himself would like to spend the intervening time, and Laurel brushed past him into the hall.

To her right a door stood open to reveal a bulky uniformed man seated at a desk, a half-finished bottle of Coke by his hand. His head lifted from the papers before him when Laurel tapped on the door and approached the desk. For a big man, he moved surprisingly quickly to his feet and lifted his brows enquiringly.

'*Señorita*?'

'I—I want to visit my father, Daniel Trent. He was

—brought here late this afternoon.'

The brows lowered suddenly in a frown. 'This is not a good time to visit the prisoners, *señorita*. If you come back tomorrow——'

Laurel lifted an impatient hand to brush her hair back from her face, and saw his expression change as his eyes followed the movement.

'Señor Trent, you said? Then you are——'

'His daughter,' Laurel inserted drily.

'—Señor Ramirez's betrothed,' he finished as if she had not spoken. His eyes were still fixed on the ring adorning her third finger ... Brent's ring. Surprise registered briefly in his close-set eyes, as if he found it hard to believe that his rich compatriot would put such paltry jewels on his beloved's finger.

Laurel fumed as she followed the stocky figure out of the room and along a passage lined with heavy dark doors. At the last one on the left, the police officer inserted a large key and turned it noisily.

'*Gracias, señor,*' she murmured as she stepped past him into the small adobe-walled room, her eyes skimming over the bare furnishings of simple cot with a rough shelf above it, to the battered table where her father sat on a slatted wood chair.

'*Laurel!*' He started up, and she ran to throw her arms round him.

'Dad! ... oh, Dad,' she murmured brokenly against his sea tanned neck, and clung to his muscular shoulders under navy knit shirt.

'I—I didn't want you coming here,' he said huskily, then pushed her away to arm's length. 'Ramirez didn't come with you?'

'Ram—? Oh. No, he—he doesn't know I'm here.'

'I'd have been surprised if he let you come to a place

like this alone.' Dan, frowning, indicated the chair he
had just risen from. 'Sit down, honey, I'll take the cot.'

When Laurel was seated, he sat on the rickety cot
and stretched out his long legs before him. Seeing her
disdainful glance round his new abode, he smiled
wryly.

'This may not be much, sweetheart, but it's a hundred per cent better than where they put me to begin
with.'

'But you shouldn't be here at all!' Laurel burst out
in a spurt of frustrated anger that covered her more
urgent need to burst into inadequate tears. She couldn't
bear to see the father she adored, the man whose every
breath had to be drawn in the freedom of sea breezes,
confided in a miserable prison cell.

'I know, honey, I know,' he soothed, lifting a hand as
if to stem the tide of her anger. 'I felt that way too
when they first brought me in, but after seeing how
some of the other people have to live here——' He
broke off and leaned forward, resting his arms on his
knees. 'Would you believe that there are Americans
and other nationalities who've been here for months
or even years before they have a chance of a trial?
Their families, lawyers—nobody can do anything for
them.'

'Well, maybe they're guilty,' Laurel cried wildly,
'but you're not! There must be some way we can persuade them to let you go!'

'Influence is all that matters around here, baby,' Dan
told her, getting up to pace restlessly round the small
room. 'They haven't found those two guys who chartered my boat yet.'

'But when they do you'll be free, once they tell the
authorities that you had nothing to do with it.'

Dan shook his head. 'Why should they help me? From the little I know of them, they wouldn't lift a finger to help their own grandmothers. We have to face it, Laurel—they'll probably say I was in it up to the neck with them.'

'But you weren't!'

He sighed heavily and came back to sit on the squeaky springs again. 'You know that, and I know that, but how do we convince anyone else?'

'I'll get Brent to come down here,' she said edgily, her hand opening and closing on the clasp of the purse on her lap. 'He'll know what to do.'

'Will he?' Dan's eyes met hers caustically, and Laurel's slid away. She knew what her father was thinking. Brent had shown an unsuspected streak of stiff-necked Puritanism when he had discovered Dan Trent's freewheeling way of life, so what chance was there of him fighting a winning case for his fiancée's father accused of drug smuggling? Laurel felt her heart sink at the thought of explaining the position to Brent.

'Well,' she said weakly, 'maybe he could recommend someone. After all, Brent's speciality is company law, so he——'

'Didn't you hear what I said?' Dan interrupted with unusual harshness. 'States side lawyers can't do anything down here. The law has to take its course.'

'But we have to do something!' Laurel gasped through a tight knot in her throat.

'Only somebody like Diego Ramirez can do anything,' Dan said savagely, beating one balled fist into the palm of his other hand. 'He has power, influence, and——' He looked directly into Laurel's eyes. 'He tells me he wants to marry you.'

'He told you that?' she asked faintly.

'In no uncertain terms.' Quietly, Dan added: 'Why didn't you tell me things had progressed that far with him? Last night at the El Mirador, you let me think he was married.'

'Did I?' Laurel cast round frantically in her mind for a solution to this new problem. If she said that she had indeed believed that Diego was married to Consuelo just the night before, how could her father believe that today she had agreed to marry him? And with burning clarity, she knew that that was exactly what she must convince Dan of. Diego was the only one who could bring pressure to bear for her father's release.

'Well, I—I guess I didn't want you to know I'd been seeing somebody else while I'm still engaged to Brent,' she said with a coyness that sounded insincere to herself, but Dan appeared to accept her statement at face value. Indeed, he seemed relieved to hear it.

'You don't know how happy I am to know that you feel that way, honey,' he leaned forward to squeeze her hand meaningfully. 'The minute I saw Ramirez last night I knew he was more the man for you than Brent could ever be. There's a certain way a man looks at the woman he loves, and that's the way Ramirez— Diego—looked at you. I always got the feeling that Brent might look at himself in the mirror that way, but——' Dan stopped abruptly and ran a broad hand over his head. 'Honey, I don't want you to think I'm saying that because I'm in this place. I'd stay here and crumble to dust before I'd let you——'

'I know, Dad,' Laurel inserted quickly. 'But—Diego —can get the wheels moving much faster if he's doing it on behalf of his f-father-in-law. He knows lots of people in the right places, so it's just a matter of time before you're out of here.' She glanced again round the depressing cellroom.

'You're sure this is what you want, Laurel?' Dan insisted, his hand tightening over hers. 'Marriage is for ever to a man like Ramirez, so if you have any doubts, now's the time to speak out. There's no guarantee I'll be released even with his help, so don't let that influence you into rushing into a marriage that isn't right for you.'

Laurel looked down at the broad hand covering hers, feeling its warmth combating the chill that had struck deep within her. 'Marriage is for ever to a man like Ramirez ...' Only after her father had spoken those words did she realise that deep down she had been planning that if the marriage took place, it would be a shortlived arrangement, terminating upon her father's release.

Still, she told herself with an inward sigh, nothing had changed. She could still leave Diego and go back to Brent. Feeling more hopeful suddenly, she looked up and gave Dan a tremulous smile.

'I've never been more sure that this is the right thing to do, Dad. All my future happiness is tied up in Diego.' And that was no lie.

For the first time, Dan Trent smiled in his relaxed way, years seeming to fall from his salty tanned features. He, too, looked buoyantly hopeful when she took her leave a few minutes later, telling Laurel silently of how much he was relying on Diego's help to gain his freedom.

CHAPTER FOUR

'*Hola!*'

After schooling herself to hear Diego's somewhat cool mid-tones, Laurel stared blankly down at the telephone. The voice at the other end was a woman's, deep and thick, so not Consuelo's.

'I—may I speak with Señor Ramirez?'

'Señor Ramirez swims in the pool. Is *importante*?'

'Yes. I'll wait.'

Making the original call with fingers trembling so hard they could scarcely dial had been bad enough. Laurel knew she could never summon up the courage to call again.

'*Momento, por favor.*'

Laurel drummed nervously on the side table and drew deep breaths as she waited for Diego to come to the phone. Who was swimming in the pool with him? Consuelo with her dark-eyed beauty? It wasn't hard to imagine that Diego, with his air of barely suppressed sensuality, appreciated the female form scantily clad in the privacy of his own pool.

The receiver was picked up at the other end, and her fingers tensed on hers as Diego announced himself.

'It's—Laurel Trent,' she said hesitantly.

'Ah.' There was silence for a moment, and Laurel wondered if it was due to the surge of satisfaction he must be feeling. His tone was level, however, when he went on: 'You have been to see your father?'

'I—yes, last night.' Laurel swallowed deeply. 'I'm

prepared to consider your offer.'

Another silence, which went on for so long that she wondered if they had been cut off. But at last Diego spoke in a controlled tone.

'Perhaps you will call me again when you make up your mind to accept my proposal.'

Laurel gasped as if he had thrown her into the pool he had just come from. After all the hours she had spent tossing and turning in her sleepless bed bringing herself to this point, the least he could have done was to meet her halfway. But that kind of understanding, compassion, was evidently outside the orbit of Diego Ramirez's nature.

'All right, damn you,' she choked, 'I'll marry you.'

If she had expected a flowery speech of loverlike protestations she was disappointed in his abrupt: 'I will be with you in thirty minutes. You are at the hotel?'

'Yes.'

'*Adios*, Laurel. Until we meet.'

The time seemed endless as she paced between one room and the other, even the scene from her balcony windows of activity on beach and water failing for once to hold her attention. Her thoughts were chaotic.

Why would a man like Diego Ramirez, wealthy, powerful, with a world of beautiful women ready to fall at his attractive feet, want to marry someone like herself? Her training as a model had given her poise, a grace of carriage, and she wasn't falsely modest about her looks—which, she supposed now, might appeal in their fairness to a man surrounded for the most part by darkly exotic women. But none of that added up to a reason for wanting to marry her. An affair, yes, such as she had suspected when she had believed him to be married. A lifelong commitment? No.

The same chill enveloped her as had pierced her insides in her father's prison cell. 'Marriage is for ever,' he had said. Laurel herself had held the same belief ever since she could remember. But here she was now contemplating that sacred state with a view to opting out when her father was released from prison.

But Diego only had himself to thank for that, she told herself fiercely as she rushed into the bedroom and feverishly applied make-up to put a false glow on her pallid cheeks. The white tailored short-sleeved dress she was wearing reflected paleness to her skin, robbing it of the little colour it had had after a sleepless night.

When the confident knock came at the outer door, she froze in her tracks. The nightmare that had begun the afternoon before with her father's arrest was far from being over. As she forced her feet across the tiled floor, Laurel knew it was only just beginning.

She was taken by surprise when Diego, dressed casually in close-fitting jeans and white rollneck sweater yet still looking expensively turned out, took her hand and pressed his lips to her palm. The gesture was foreign to her, and a little distasteful, so she pulled her hand away abruptly.

'Don't do that,' she said sharply. 'It's not necessary.'

His brows lifted in a black arc. 'You consider it unnecessary to receive such a small symbol of my devotion?'

Laughing voices echoed in the corridor and Laurel said jerkily: 'You'd better come in,' turning back into the small living room with its Spanish decor.

'Let's get it straight from the beginning,' she said tautly, turning again to face the eyes that were like banked fires in his olive-toned face. 'I've agreed to marry you for one reason, and one reason only. You know what that reason is. So don't let's have any false displays of affection.'

'I never display affection falsely, *querida*,' he told her with dangerous softness. Then, his eyes cooling, he gestured to the small bar next to the kitchenette. 'May I pour us some drinks? A little celebration is perhaps in order.'

'I'm not in the mood to celebrate, *señor*,' Laurel said drily, 'but I do feel the need for a strong whisky and soda.'

He brought the drinks to where she stood at the balcony doors envying the carefree couples cavorting on the beach. She and Brent might have come here for their honeymoon ...

'Thank you,' she said coolly, accepting the half-filled glass Diego handed to her.

'A toast to—a fruitful marriage,' he raised his glass, then, when Laurel showed no signs of following suit, tipping it up to swallow deeply of its contents.

'If you mean what I think you mean,' Laurel told him frostily, 'you can forget it. This marriage is to be one in name only, so don't build up your hopes for a yearly influx of tiny Ramirezes!'

For a moment he was still, then with a toss of his wrist he emptied his glass and set it down on the table beside them.

'No, *querida*,' he shook his head with maddening certitude, 'this marriage cannot be in name only. I will take only one wife in my lifetime, and she will be the mother of my children. You, Laurel.'

Laurel gulped on her drink before seeking his eyes. 'Why?' she asked brokenly. 'Why do you want to marry

me? We hardly know each other, let alone—love.
We've hardly even kissed . . .'

'That can be remedied at any time,' he said softly,
reaching a hand up to touch the silver cascade of her
hair, which she had left loose in an access of despair
before his arrival. His touch disturbed her, heralding
as it did the threat of further intimacies she would be
powerless to prevent if they were indissolubly linked
in a marriage relationship. Vaguely, as from a distance,
she heard the muted sounds of his voice, and together
with the whisky she had swallowed so rapidly they
formed a hypnotic effect on her senses.

'Have you never met someone for the first time,
Laurel, and felt you had known them for all eternity?
That somewhere in another time, another place, two
souls had been intertwined and that it was their destiny to meet again, to love again? That is how I felt
the first time I saw you, Laurel, at a fashion show in
Acapulco, and I knew that you were the woman I had
waited for all these years.'

Mesmerized by the soft persuasion in his voice,
Laurel's eyes clung to the liquid darkness of his before
being drawn irresistibly to the masterfully drawn outline of his lips. She felt the glass being removed gently
from her hand, a deceptively gentle arm at her back
pressing her forward.

Diego's first kiss held even less fire than Brent's undemanding lovemaking, and Laurel felt a distinct pang
of disappointment. There was only the familiar sensation of warmth as the male mouth pressed against
the softness of hers, teasing lightly at the corners. The
punishing kiss he had extracted from her at El Mirador had held much more excitement, provocation, although it had been administered from anger.

Then, with a suddenness that left her breathless, Diego was murmuring brokenly at her ear, his lips trailing hotly from there to her closed lids, her cheek, and finally closing possessively over her mouth.

No man, not even Brent, had kissed her in that way and she instinctively stiffened, pushing with her hands against the male implacability of his chest, only to find her attention distracted by the expert touch of his hands. They seemed to be everywhere, stroking, caressing, cajoling with a sensitivity of their own in their knowledge of what would please her woman's body. She had never been so conscious of her female curves and contours until Diego's hands cupped, smoothed and pressed them to the throbbing male warmth of his. Her drugged senses were aware only of a primitive need to give without reserve to the man of her choice.

But Diego wasn't the man of her choice. That remembrance came with the sear of her indrawn breath when his mouth lifted from hers. The soft murmur of his voice at her ear suddenly repelled her and she pushed herself from the confinement of his arms and backed against the kitchenette counter, her eyes a fathomless sea green as she stared at him, denying the recognition her pounding heart insisted on.

'I—I don't feel that way about you,' she gasped, moving away from his compelling aura, elucidating for his incredulous stare: 'I mean—all that stuff about —being fated from other lives. That doesn't mean anything to me.'

'No?' He moved with silent tread to stand near her again. Her darting eyes saw a faint film of perspiration on his brow, the flare of his nostrils, and sickness churned in her stomach. 'Yet you are not indifferent to me, *cariña*,' he added huskily, raising a hand to

twist a strand of her hair between his fingers. 'Our
marriage has much to recommend it.'

Laurel jerked woodenly away from him. 'A marriage
between us, *señor*, has only one thing to recommend
it in my eyes, and that is the release of my father.'

'So. The sooner we are married the sooner I will be
in a position to help him reach that goal.' Taking his
glass in one hand, he gestured to Laurel's and when
she shook her head, strode over to the bar. 'You realise
that I cannot guarantee his freedom,' he went quietly
from there, 'only a speeding up of his trial. If he is
innocent——'

'Of course he's innocent!' Laurel swung round scath-
ingly. 'My father has never done a dishonest thing in
his life, let alone become involved in the drug trade!'

'Yet he appears to have no business, no profession?'

'He—gave that up after my mother died.' Laurel
swivelled back to the window, hiding the tears brought
on by sleeplessness and the unbelievable events of the
past twenty-four hours. 'He—just seemed to want to
get away from everything that reminded him of——'

'And this included you, his daughter?' Diego interrupted from the sofa, where he had taken his drink.

Laurel shook her head impatiently. 'He had to put
me in school. What else could a widowed man do with
a twelve-year-old daughter? I could hardly share his
life on the boat.'

'It would not have been right for a young girl,' he
agreed with such alacrity that Laurel sensed that he
knew all about the women who had filled her father's
loneliness temporarily. And that made her wonder
about the women in Diego's life, the ones who had
given him such sureness in his lovemaking. They must
have been legion, she thought abstractly, her eyes flit-

ting over his smoothly knit frame on the sofa.

'Come and sit down, *querida*,' he instructed, patting the sofa as if reading her thoughts. Contrarily, Laurel took the chair in juxtaposition to the couch.

'How long do you think it will be before my father's trial comes up?' she asked, ignoring his wince of distaste at her businesslike tone.

'I cannot say at this moment,' he shrugged. 'Perhaps one month, perhaps two.'

'Months!'

'Under other circumstances,' his mouth twisted into a wry smile, 'your father could be imprisoned for many months, perhaps years.'

'I know. My father told me that last night. Well,' briskly, 'how soon can the marriage take place?'

'Such eagerness on the part of my bride!' Diego got suddenly to his feet, looking like a smooth and slightly dangerous jungle animal as he paced around the small room. 'The wedding must be held in Mexico City. I have many friends and business acquaintances who would be less than happy if they were not invited to witness the ceremony. Apart from Consuelo, my close family consists only of my grandmother, who lives at the family estate in Cuernavaca. She is very old, and unlikely to travel to Mexico City for the occasion.'

Laurel felt a faint tug of surprise at his mention of family ... apart from his dead brother, she had somehow imagined him a man alone without a past or discernible future.

'You have no parents?'

'No more.' A glance up into his face revealed a taut line to his lips, a perceptible hardening of his jaw. 'Both were killed in a plane travelling back from your

State of Kansas many years ago. I was fourteen years old.'

'I'm sorry.' Strangely, the words were more than perfunctory. Hadn't Laurel herself gone through the trauma of losing one parent? To lose both in one fell swoop must have been agony for a young boy.

But Diego shrugged. 'The young recover quickly. And now,' he came back to seat himself on the sofa, pinning her eyes to his with his liquid black stare, 'we must settle a date for the nuptials. I will arrange for the civil ceremony a week from now—or perhaps next Friday, the religious rites to be conducted the following day, Saturday. It is perhaps not possible at such short notice to be married in the Cathedral, but perhaps a side chapel ...' He seemed to have forgotten Laurel's presence, lost as he was in the details of arranging a speedy marriage.

'That—isn't very much time,' she inserted drily, moistening her lips with a nervous tongue.

'The sooner you are my wife, the better it will be,' he brushed away her objection almost brusquely. 'It would not, of course, be correct for you to stay at my town house in Mexico City, so you will go directly to Consuelo's home there.'

'No!' Laurel bit off sharply. 'I—I want to stay close to my father. Why can't we be married here in Acapulco?' Hysterically, she wondered at her own sudden acceptance of the inevitability of a marriage between herself and a man she scarcely knew. Didn't want to know.

A frown she was beginning to recognise as peculiarly his slashed two lines between his brows. 'That would not be possible, for your sake as much as for mine. Some of the people I will be contacting about your father's case will attend the ceremony in Mexico City, but not here.' One olive hand came out to clasp the hand in her lap. 'If you wish, we can come here immediately after the ceremony and spend our honeymoon at Jacintha Point. In that way, you will be able to visit your father daily.'

With that Laurel had to be content, although before Diego left she was able to persuade him that two days spent with Consuelo would be sufficient to purchase bridal accoutrements. To his suggestion that she charge everything to the accounts he held in every major store in Mexico City she could only agree. Her slender bank balance would scarcely run to the finery befitting the bride of one of Mexico's most prominent men. The unwilling bride.

CHAPTER FIVE

LAUREL pressed trembling fingers to her throbbing temples, willing herself to close out the steady hum of voices from the salon on the floor below.

The antique lace of her wedding gown seemed to weigh down her slender figure like a sapling bending to the wind, and she sank down on the padded stool before an ornately mirrored dressing table, resting her elbows on the glassed top, her hands still pressing against the pulses at her temples.

Around her the bedroom, although it was large and overwhelmingly ostentatious, seemed to close round her claustrophobically. Tall mirrored doors enclosing spacious closets reflected the monstrously large bed positioned at the far side of the room between high narrow windows. A bed whose high lofted mattresses were covered by a woven spread in an Aztec design of dark red and gold, colours which lent emphasis to the heavy black Spanish bedroom furniture and were echoed in the weighty drapes edging the windows.

A fitting decor for the Mexican wife of Diego Cesar Davis Ramirez ... Laurel had raised her brows upon hearing an English name interspersed with the Spanish during the service, but Diego had later told her briefly that his mother had been an American like herself.

This room would welcome his bride of Spanish extraction. To herself it had an alien air, a secretiveness far removed from the openness of her American upbringing. Had Diego's American mother lain in that bed, conceived her firstborn son there?

The thought sent a shudder through her, and she almost welcomed the intrusion of Consuelo, who came into the room without knocking.

'Diego has sent me to hurry you up,' she said with an insolence Laurel had become accustomed to after spending two nights under her roof. '*Dios!* You have not yet taken off the wedding dress! You are not eager to be alone with your husband?'

Her busy fingers began to unbutton the long line of small satin orbs reaching down Laurel's back. The dress had been made in a time long before the age of zippers, having been fashioned for Diego's grandmother sixty-five years before. The old lady, at her flower-filled estate in Cuernavaca, had insisted on Laurel wearing her own wedding dress.

'I have long dreamed of Diego's bride wearing the dress that was made for me when I married his grandfather,' she had told Laurel in surprisingly good English. Snapping black eyes, undimmed from her eighty-two years, had approved Laurel's slender form. 'No one in our family has been able to fit into it until now.'

Consuelo now looked enviously at the oyster satin skirt suit hanging at one side of the dressing table. Jealousy had marked each moment they had been together at the dark girl's home, so much that Laurel had welcomed even Diego's presence to offset the stifling atmosphere.

'You are lucky to have married a man as rich as Diego, I think,' she said now in her childlike voice which nevertheless held a hint of contempt.

'You could say that luck had something to do with it,' Laurel returned wryly, stripping the old lace wedding dress from her and hanging it carefully away in its wrappings. Used as she was to the easygoing atmosphere of the fashion world, she felt no selfconsciousness as she removed the floor-length underslip and stood in brief panties and scanty bra before the other girl's critical gaze.

'I do not know why Diego chose a scrawny chicken like you for his wife,' Consuelo disparaged. 'His women have always had beautiful figures, like so.' She sketched the outline of curves even more voluptuous than her own.

'Really!' Laurel fastened the waistband of the oyster skirt round her indented waist and reached for the jacket. 'It's strange that he didn't think of marrying one of them, then.'

'He has this—this——' Consuelo waved her hands helplessly, 'craze to replace the mother he lost when he was a boy. He is—how would you say?—fixed on her image.'

A fixation? Diego? A chill crept over Laurel's skin as she remembered the portrait of a fair woman between the swarthy-skinned men on the staircase a few steps away from the master bedroom. True, there was a slight surface resemblance to herself in the woman's fairness, but to suggest that a man like Diego——

'You're being fanciful,' she dismissed briskly, seating herself before the mirror to repair the make-up she had applied earlier in the day.

'No, I am not,' Consuelo returned fiercely. 'If it were so, then would he not have married me? It is a custom that when a brother dies his unmarried brother will take his widow for a wife.'

So that was the problem! Consuelo had been nourishing hopes, based on tradition, that Diego would

make her his wife after a suitable mourning period had
passed. Instead, he had taken a foreigner, a woman
with no understanding of those customs. Laurel wished
with all her heart that she could tell Consuelo that the
marriage was likely to be shortlived. It would last only
as long as her father's imprisonment lasted. She had no
feeling of compunction about it. Diego, in forcing her
into a marriage she wanted no part of, could expect no
more.

'You should have asked Diego about that a long
time ago,' she now told the fiery-eyed Consuelo.

'Asked me what?' his voice came lazily from the door.

Laurel looked round quickly from the dressing table
to see him saunter towards them, leanly handsome in
the dark suit he had worn for the wedding. The carnation at his buttonhole reflected the deep fire in his
dark eyes, the glow that had been there during the
ceremony which had made them man and wife.

However much Laurel had made up her mind to
accept the marriage as a transient thing, an occurrence
necessitated only by her father's imprisonment, the
solemn air of sanctification in the church had had its
effect on her. The ceremony had held all the elements
she had dreamed of as a girl growing up in the convent
... the massed flowers adorning the altar, the hushed
air of solemnity as the service proceeded, the darkly
handsome man at her side promising to love and
cherish her. Her own responses were given in a voice
made low and vibrant by the awesomeness of the
occasion, and when her eyes met the dark lustre in
Diego's she wished for a fleeting moment that the ceremony was one that united them not only in fact but
in spirit.

The rest was a daze in her mind, the cool touch of

Diego's lips on hers in a sealing kiss, the triumphal march from the chapel, the smiling faces of Diego's friends surrounding them at either side.

Then back at the palatial Ramirez town home, where the spacious salon easily accommodated the hundred or so guests, and where prosperous men of business took advantage of the situation to kiss Laurel's smooth cheeks, their wives looking on with frank curiosity. To Laurel, their speculation was preferable to the somewhat venomous looks cast in her direction by their daughters, some of whom were petulantly plain while others had all the fire and dark-eyed beauty of their Spanish blood.

Now Diego said a few short words in Spanish to his brother's widow, and with a shrug she went from the room, closing the door loudly behind her.

Diego's burning eyes met Laurel's in the dressing table mirror.

'So, *mi esposa*, for the first time we are alone. I have had to endure the sight of other men's lips on your skin until I wanted to carry you away to Jacintha Point before courtesy permitted.'

His own lips had descended to the nape of her neck, where they teased lightly at that sensitive point, sending curious sensations along Laurel's spine so that she shivered convulsively and gave a strangled: 'Don't!' With the word she brought her head round and unwittingly exposed the soft tremble of her mouth to the marauding assault of his.

There was nothing tentative about the pressure of lips that crushed hers and opened possessively in an instant passion which forced her own unwilling mouth into acquiescence. The awkward turn of her body on the dressing stool permitted only the ineffective lift of her nerveless hands to his chest, where they lay paralysed against the fine cloth of his jacket.

Then as if his mouth held the power of a flaming torch, a response frightening in its intensity was ignited deep within her and swept aside every inhibition she had ever had. Nothing had ever seemed more natural than that she should be straining up like this to deepen the kiss between them, or that Diego should slide her impatiently off the stool and draw her up to meet the vibrant curve of his body. Triumphant possession was in the touch of his lips to the faint hollows of her throat, the sureness of his fingers as they undid the top buttons of her jacket and slid inside to cup the urgent swelling of her breast.

'*Te adoro,*' he murmured against the silky skin of her cheek. 'Must we wait until we reach Jacintha Point?' He pulled away from her then to regard her with eyes burning deep with the passion that still held his body in its sway. Gently his thumb rubbed lightly over her cheekbone, and he quizzed huskily: 'Shall I send them all away so that we can be alone, *querida*?'

His reminder of the guests milling in the salon below was enough to still Laurel's racing pulses to a more normal rate and clear the swirling desire from her limbs. Stepping abruptly away from his unsuspecting arms, she turned her back to him and refastened the buttons of her jacket with trembling fingers.

'No!' she choked. 'No matter what you tell them, it won't make this marriage any more real. I told you it was to be in n-name only.'

Her shoulders were gripped and spun fiercely until her startled eyes met the suddenly harsh cast in Diego's.

'And I told you, *querida*, that our marriage is for all time. From our coming together children will be born, sinew of my sinew, flesh of your flesh. *Our* children, Laurel.'

'No!'

Diego's expression softened slightly. 'How can you say no?' he chided, his hand sliding down to cover the wild throb of her heart. 'You want this joining as much as I. Listen to your heartbeat, and know that mine beats even stronger for you.'

The words would have sounded overly dramatic from an American man, yet from Diego they held a kind of inevitability that sent fear shivering momentarily through her. As the fire he had aroused in her veins subsided, so cool reason took over. What woman wouldn't have been carried away by the passionate expertise of a deadly attractive man? A Latin man, far removed from the homely familiarity of Brent and the breezy non-insistence of his kisses.

'You're living in a fantasy world, *señor*,' she told him coolly, breaking from him to pick up the tortoiseshell comb from the dresser and rearrange the fine strands of her hair ruffled by his lovemaking. 'You know why I married you, and the reason certainly isn't the perpetuation of the Ramirez house. As soon as my father is released, I'll——' She broke off abruptly and bit her lip.

'You will what, *cariña*?' Diego inserted with dangerous softness, his fingers running down the silk of her sleeve to clasp her wrist and swing her in a half arc to face him again. 'You think I have proclaimed you my wife before my friends and associates, only to have you shame me as soon as my usefulness has ended? No, my wife, I will make sure that you remain mine for all time.'

Laurel shivered as her eyes met the fiery glitter in

his. There could be no mistaking the forceful intent
of his words, although they were spoken so quietly. It
needed little imagination on her part, either, to guess
the direction of his thoughts. By forcing her into wifely
submission, and perhaps giving her a child, he was
assuming that an annulment would no longer be possible.

In his devout eyes that was no doubt true, but in an
enlightened world all things were possible, including
divorce, child or no child.

After retouching her lips with the lipstick he had
kissed away, she sighed and picked up her purse from
the dressing table. She rose, slim and elegant, to face
Diego.

'I'm ready,' she said quietly.

For a moment he regarded her broodingly, then his
hand came out to curve round her elbow. 'Then we
can leave. Our luggage has already been taken to the
car.'

'You're not changing?' she asked, surprised.

A faint smile touched his stormy mouth. 'The servants at Jacintha Point were unable to attend the ceremony. They will appreciate seeing me, at least, in my
wedding finery.' Sarcasm edged his voice as he raised a
hand to caress her cheek with his fingertips. 'Besides, I
want everyone we pass to know that I have today
acquired a beautiful bride. It will give them pleasure
to think of the wedding night to come.'

'Then the pleasure is all theirs,' Laurel responded
tartly, pausing at the head of the winding stairway
when Diego's grip tightened on her elbow.

'For your father's sake, if not for mine, try to act
like a loving bride before my friends.'

The veiled threat stayed with Laurel as they des-

cended the stairs together, her fairness compellingly
contrasted with his darkness. The guests, grouped
round the softly playing fountain at the centre of the
coolly tiled hall, fell silent when they caught sight of
the wedding couple, then they surged forward to the
foot of the stairs, jocularly calling good wishes that
were as bold as the amount of fine champagne they had
drunk.

Diego's arm slid round Laurel's waist, halting her in
mid step half way down the staircase. His hand turned
her forcibly to face him and, smiling, he commanded
her softly to kiss him.

'No!' she breathed indignantly, glancing down at
the upturned expectant faces.

'Do it,' he hissed fiercely, and tightened his hold until her body was pressed intimately to his.

Shouts of encouragement in Spanish and English
seemed to propel Laurel's face upward in an automatic gesture, her lips brushing lightly against Diego's.
But when she would have pulled away, his hands came
up to spread across her hair at the back and her mouth
was imprisoned by the warm audacity of his. She
moaned in muffled protest when his tongue flicked
impudently over the sensitive inner surface of her lips,
and when at last he raised his head, a sardonic glitter
at the back of his eyes, she looked as ruffled as he had
intended. The pale flush on her cheeks could as easily
be mistaken for a bride's modesty at revealing her love
as for the anger that had actually caused it.

Diego himself, once they were out of sight of the
wellwishers, lapsed into a contained silence, his sole
concentration on driving the sleek silver Mercedes at a
rapid pace through the city and on the highway whose
terminus was Acapulco. To the occasional driver who

recognised his newly married status and to the peasants working in the fields bordering the highway, he raised a hand in salute, but limited his conversation with Laurel to noncommittal comments about the areas they passed through.

And that was fine with her, she thought as she settled back into the sumptuous leather upholstery of her seat. It was ironic that she should be sitting next to a man she might, in other circumstances, have regarded as her ideal. Apart from sharing the faith that had always meant so much to her, Diego Ramirez had all the good looks, wealth and position a girl might dream of. He made love with a natural eagerness unknown to a man like Brent Halliday—her ex-fiancé.

Her eyes went to the glowing emerald surrounded by flawless diamonds adorning her ring hand above the slender gold span of her wedding ring. It was Diego himself who had removed Brent's ring as if it were a paltry trinket and told her to send it back to him. As if Brent could be brushed aside by the penning of a few lines of apology, Laurel asking his forgiveness for falling in love with another man so precipitously. There had been no time for a reply to her letter, and she wondered if Brent would read between the lines of her stilted letter and know that her heart still belonged to him. She had skimmed lightly over her father's predicament, telling him that there had been a mistake which would be straightened out immediately.

'What are you thinking of so pensively?' Diego broke into her thoughts, shattering her vision of Brent and the familiar environs of Los Angeles and bringing her back abruptly to the opulent car her new husband drove so competently.

'I was thinking about Brent, my fiancé,' she told him

bluntly, her mouth firming to still the sudden wave of homesickness that threatened her composure.

After a brief pause while Diego skirted a broken down farm wagon on the road, he said with a faint frown: 'You have no fiancé, Laurel. You have a husband, and in just a few hours you will become a wife in every way, not just in name as you persist in thinking. This Brent,' he paused again to negotiate a curve, 'would he not have made you his wife tonight if he and not I had been your bridegroom?'

'Not if I hadn't wanted to become his wife,' Laurel returned tautly, stifling the sob that rose to her throat.

'Then it is as I suspected,' he said with complacent dryness. 'Ice-water flows in his veins, not the hot blood of a man.'

'Brent is as much of a man as you'll ever be,' she bridled quickly in defence. 'The only difference between you is that he's civilised and—and gentle—undemanding ...' Diego cast her a sardonic sideways glance as she floundered to a stop.

'If all men had been such as you describe this Brent, then civilisation would have come to a halt long ago. Do you think that the *conquistadores* played cat and mouse with the women they desired? No. When they saw a woman who pleased them they took her. And the women they took were never known to complain.'

'Would anyone have listened?' Laurel queried bitterly.

'Perhaps not,' he conceded, lean hands confident at the wheel. 'But few of them took the ultimate road to freedom, which would have been death. Instead they founded families such as my own, loving their children as passionately as their husbands loved them. They were the real women, Laurel, the ones who recognised their fate and accepted it.'

'The range of choice wasn't all that wide, was it?' she mocked, and Diego made no reply to that.

They were descending now to the mountain-ringed Bay of Acapulco, and the glittering spectacle appeared to hold him as much in its thrall as it did Laurel. But in her case, the palm-fringed shores of pale gold faded into insignificance at the thought that soon she would be seeing her father again.

The long, winding drive that curved round the tropical gardens of the Jacintha Point estate was unfamiliar to Laurel. On her one brief visit to Diego's resort home they had arrived by sea from Acapulco, a trip made smooth by the superbly constructed motor yacht which was obviously Diego's pride and joy.

Coming on the house in that way had brought a gasp of admiration from Laurel despite her reluctance to see any part of the life of the man who had virtually blackmailed her into marriage. The house held a commanding position on the cliff top and stretched almost from side to side of the Point, descending in three-storied layers in a cascade of white walls and thick red Spanish-tiled roofs. From balconies spouted froths of brilliant blossoms in orange, red, mauve, and when they had ascended the steps from the beach to the house area Laurel had drawn in her breath again at the teeming plant life studded with colour on the wide terrace bordering the cliff's edge.

Now, as Diego guided the car along the drive to the front of the house, she realised that someone approaching it from this side would be totally unimpressed by its size, not realising that most of the living areas tumbled down the hillside behind.

Black-arched double doors were thrown open as the car drew to a stop, and Laurel recognised the plump figure of Juanita, Diego's housekeeper, backed by her tall and lean husband, Carlos, who seemed to be a general factotum at the villa.

Juanita, her dark-skinned face wreathed in smiles, came forward to welcome them, her black button eyes delightedly taking in Diego's formal clothes, the carnation still fresh-looking in his buttonhole. While Diego bent to kiss her on each cheek, she murmured something in unintelligible Spanish and he glanced immediately at Laurel, dark eyes glinting.

'You must ask my bride tomorrow if I am the perfect groom, Juanita,' he said in the same language, and Laurel's skin grew pink. Even had she not understood the language, there was no mistaking the meaning.

After a sincere handshake from Carlos, Diego put a hand under Laurel's elbow, urging her towards the house's cool interior and ordering that light refreshments be brought to them in the small *sala*. Laurel was unable to summon more than a stiff smile in answer to the housekeeper's words of welcome, and her legs felt wooden as Diego led her across the smaller upper hall and down six steps to the polished-tile main hall, which seemed to be a central core for the rooms leading off it.

On her first visit most of the time had been spent in the large room to their right, furnished comfortably with sofas and chairs meant to convey a vacation atmosphere. But now Diego steered her towards a smaller, more intimate sitting room where deep cushioned armchairs and couches were arranged to take advantage of the stupendous sea views from wall-to-wall windows. Potted palms and slender-leaved dracaenas gave off the atmosphere of a tropical greenhouse, and Laurel undid the top two buttons of her jacket as she broke away from Diego's grip and went to stand before the windows.

The ocean swelled and creamed at the outermost tip of the Point, dividing round it to form two separate beaches, one rough and wild as the rollers broke directly from the open sea, the other magically protected by a line of jagged rocks in the distance.

Sensing Diego's presence at her shoulder, Laurel murmured abstractedly: 'At least I'll be able to swim here.'

He seemed about to say something in harsh response, then change it to: 'It is safe to swim only at the south beach; the undertow is too powerful to the north. But it is safest of all to swim in the pool, and more convenient.'

Convenient? Who thought of convenience when a travel agent's dream beach of curving white sand edged a sea of translucent green? Coconut palms ringed the beaches in an irregular pattern, their almost ripened fruits clustered at their centres.

She felt Diego's warm hand on the nape of her neck, the fingers of his other hand reaching for her chin to tilt her head towards him. For a moment her eyes were caught in the unguarded expression on his face, then her lashes fell like a shutter over her eyes.

'You think that swimming is all you will enjoy at Jacintha Point, *querida*?' he put softly, his fingers tightening on the rounded flesh of her jawbones. 'I can promise you, *mi esposa*, that swimming will be only one small part of your pleasure.'

Laurel jerked her head sideways away from his touch. 'You're very sure of yourself, *señor*.'

'In the matter of pleasing my wife, yes,' he returned blandly, his voice growing husky. '*Cariña*, you will forget this Brent of yours when I hold you in my arms tonight, when I worship you with my body as I vowed today at our wedding.'

Laurel turned restlessly back to the window. 'You disgust me, *señor*,' she said coldly. 'How can you speak of such things when you know our marriage was a farce? God forgive me, I took sacred vows today to a man I don't love, for my father's sake. Don't compound my error by forcing me to—to——'

A startled cry escaped her when Diego whipped her round to face him, all gentleness gone from his smooth olive features.

'You say you have no love for me, yet the kisses we have shared tell me the opposite. You think you will not grow to love me as your husband once you are completely mine?' His dark eyes softened, and his voice dropped a notch or two. 'I am sorry, *niña*. It is only natural that you feel a little fear, but can you not trust me to be gentle, to respect the innocence you have guarded?'

It was on the tip of Laurel's tongue to ask how he could be so certain she had guarded her 'innocence' in that particular respect, but Juanita bustled in at that moment bearing a laden tray. Her bright eyes darted momentarily to where Diego and his new wife stood close together at the windows, noting in one swift scrutiny Laurel's flushed cheeks and the loosened buttons at the neck of her jacket.

Laurel turned away with an irritated frown, and it was Diego who thanked the housekeeper.

'*Gracias*, Juanita.' He added a few rapid-fire words in Spanish, something to do with the unpacking of the

Señora's clothes, and she nodded vigorously before leaving the room.

Diego turned back and said courteously: 'Will you pour tea for us, Laurel?'

About to object, Laurel shrugged her shoulders instead and moved to the low table where the tray had been set. She was hot and thirsty after the long drive, and she had little energy left for sparring with the man she was beginning to fear and hate. Far better that she conserve her spirit for the confrontation she knew would come later that evening. She was more certain than ever that Diego Ramirez would come no closer to the intimate parts of her than he had already. Somehow she would make sure of that, although in all honesty she had to admit that her unschooled senses were too openly vulnerable to a personality like his. Everything about him was exotic, from the pure sensuality emanating from his body to the opulence of his surroundings.

Surprisingly, Diego kept the atmosphere relaxed by speaking informally of other things than their ill-conceived marriage. Accepting the fine china cup from Laurel's slender fingers, he sat opposite her in a comfortably upholstered armchair, crossing one leg over the other, helping himself liberally to the daintily prepared sandwiches and rich creamy small cakes after Laurel had professed herself uninterested in them.

'Did you know, Laurel, that this estate is named after my grandmother?'

'I hadn't thought about it,' she replied coolly, drinking thirstily from the small cup and replenishing it immediately.

'Jacintha is my grandmother's name, and when my father had this place built he named it for her.'

'Not for his wife?' she asked with pointed sarcasm, and was surprised to see a look of pain cross his eyes.

'My grandmother did not approve his marriage to my mother,' he said stiffly. 'She was an American, alien to our customs and standards of behaviour.'

Laurel silently applauded the long dead ——

'What was your mother's name?'

There was a fractionary pause before Diego replied cursorily: 'Laura. Her name before marriage was Laura Davis.'

A cold shaft struck Laurel in her midriff section. Had Consuelo been right after all in her assertion that Diego had married her, Laurel, because of her similarity to his mother? The mother he had lost at a vulnerable age for a boy. There was something eerie in the thought that even the names were similar, and Laurel shivered. Diego noticed the sudden tremor and frowned as he looked searchingly at her.

'What is it, *querida*?' he asked softly, uncrossing his legs and leaning towards her. 'You cannot think that my grandmother looks on you in the same light. Would she have welcomed you as she did, let you wear her bridal gown, if she did not accept you as a fitting wife for me?'

Laurel set down her cup and rose quickly to her feet. 'I really don't care very much whether your grandmother accepts me or not,' she said coldly, knowing as she spoke the words that they were untruthful. In reality she had quite liked the autocratic old lady with the snapping black eyes who had shown by her every word and look how much she idolised Diego, her only remaining grandson. 'May I go to my room now?'

'I will take you to our suite,' Diego corrected matter-of-factly, rising in one fluid motion and coming to join.

her. 'Juanita is preparing a special dinner in our honour, but it will not be served until eight-thirty, so
there is plenty of time.'

Plenty of time for what? Laurel wondered wildly as
she followed him across the tiled hall to a passage on
the same level. Time to fulfil his threats of becoming
her husband in entirety?

Diego opened the door into a lavish set of rooms
which were virtually a separate apartment from the
rest of the house. Double doors were thrown open off
an inner hallway to reveal an enormous master
bedroom sumptuously yet tastefully furnished and
decorated. The full-length windows gave on to a
flower-filled balcony overlooking the wild north cove,
and a wide-spanned bed dominated one wall. The Ramirez men, Laurel thought involuntarily, liked plenty
of room to exercise their matrimonial expertise. This
thought was enough to turn her round impulsively to
face Diego.

'If dinner isn't until eight-thirty, then I would like
to go and visit my father,' she said firmly, her nostrils
flaring when Diego gave a half regretful shake of his
black head.

'That is not possible today, *querida*.' He seemed
genuinely mystified at her proposal and Laurel fumed:

'Why isn't it? Our agreement was——'

'Our agreement was that you would marry me and
thereby give me greater power to hasten your father's
court case,' he bit off curtly. 'And this I will do on behalf of my wife, as I have promised.'

'You made no stipulation that I wouldn't be allowed
to see my father!'

'No such stipulation was intended,' he agreed dis-
passionately. 'But it will be expected that my new wife

will not want to be parted from me on our wedding night. Would your father expect you to leave your husband at such a time in order to visit with him?'

'Why wouldn't he? He knows that——' Laurel stopped abruptly and bit her lip. Her father didn't know that this was no love match, as Diego now pointed out to her.

'Your father knows only that I love his daughter above all other women, and that my greatest wish is to bring her happiness.'

All other women! Surely he had excluded, if only mentally, the mother he still idolised in his heart. Weary suddenly, Laurel turned away from him into the lavishly appointed bedroom with its atmosphere of light and brightness. Who would know, apart from the servants, if she went to visit her father that night? Was Diego really concerned for the opinion of his househelp, or did he want to make sure that she made no bid for escape before he had set his seal of possession on her?

'Then if I can't go to my father, I'd like to rest,' she said shortly, stepping across the whisper-soft carpet of azure blue to stand before the wide windows. Even through the closed panes she could hear the rising crescendo and withdrawal of the restless waves on the rocks.

To her surprise, Diego said formally: 'As you wish. You will find everything you require for your comfort, I think. I will return at eight to escort you to the small *sala* for drinks. Rest well, *cariña*.'

His departure was noiseless, and the headache that had bothered her earlier in the day returned to plague her, and Laurel sought in her purse for the aspirin she always carried with her. She had cast off her heeled shoes as soon as Diego had disappeared, and now she padded across the floor to the bathroom.

The elegantly appointed first section consisting of mirrored vanity unit and double gold-tapped sinks, from one of which she drew water to swallow her aspirins, led to a larger room reminiscent of a Roman bath house with its sunken green marble tub edged with potted palms, the drooping fronds of one conceal-ing a mechanised swirl attachment. The vision of soothing stimulation was too much to resist, and she hurried back to the bedroom, undoing her jacket as she went.

A door next to the bathroom opened to a massive walk-in closet where the clothes Juanita had unpacked for her were hung neatly on the right-hand rack. A man's neatly pressed suits, jackets and slacks adorned the left and that, more than anything else, forced recognition on her that Diego Ramirez was indeed her husband, had the right to have his clothes hanging in close proximity to hers, the right to ——

Blindly she reached for her white satin robe and fled from the closet. But even as the pleasantly warm water massaged her tense muscles in the marble tub, her brain was searching for ways of circumventing Diego's plans for that night. Screams would bring no more than an amused chuckle from the robust Juanita and her husband, Carlos. They would be more surprised if a bride did not display nervous jitters on her wedding night. In any case, their home was in a cottage on the grounds and it was doubtful if they would hear cries for help.

She could dress after her bath and slip out of the house, taking Diego's car as far as Acapulco, but what then? Her father would still be imprisoned in an at-

mosphere abhorrent to his freedom-loving nature, and
without Diego's help it was likely he would remain
there for months, if not years.

Sighing, lethargic, she rose from the tub and towel-
led herself dry with one of the voluminous bath sheets
before sliding into the clinging silk of her robe. Perhaps Diego's better nature could be appealed to. After
all, it couldn't gratify a man's senses apart from the
sexual to take a woman against her will.

She hesitated only for a moment before lying on top
of the floral bedspread and stretching her relaxed
muscles. She had to think of a way to hold Diego off,
if only for that night. A wry smile touched her lips
when she likened her situation to that of the slave
girl who had staved off death for a thousand and one
nights by telling the Sultan stories of such excitement
that he couldn't bear not to hear the end of them.

But somehow she fancied that Diego would not be
so easily misled from his purpose....

CHAPTER SIX

WHEN she awoke, the room was in dusky darkness and for a moment or two Laurel could remember nothing of where she was or why she was there. It was only when she heard a door open and a light switch clicked on that remembrance rushed back to overwhelm her.

The sight of Diego, startlingly handsome in white dinner jacket, coming towards the bed with the easy stride of a superbly fit man set up a panicked beating of her heart, but she was powerless to move as he came to look thoughtfully down at her. Her eyes clung hynotically to his as their liquid gaze went down to where the silk edges of her gown had parted between her breasts.

She watched sleepily as he eased himself on to the bed, his hand checking her lethargic movement to cover herself. Light from the twin bedside lamps cast a midnight sheen on his black hair as his head bent without haste to nuzzle the soft pink tip of her left breast, the mobile warmth of his lips bringing it to trembling awareness of his male persuasion. Almost absently, Laurel's hand lifted to stroke through the thick darkness of his hair, feeling its vibrant life under her fingers, opening herself to the insidious longing his lips provoked.

When his head lifted his eyes held the fiery glints of a man aroused, his voice strained to the point of hoarseness when he murmured: 'You are so beautiful, *cara*.' His fingertips trailed fire across her cheek to her throat

and along the tracery of her collarbone. Vague prick-
lings of warning stirred at the back of her mind, but
when she opened her mouth to protest weakly Diego's
lips came down hard in a kiss that made coherent
thought slide away into oblivion. There was only the
clamour of senses unfamiliar with the overwhelming
need to give, and take, and give again until she was
drained of all feeling.

His weight was pressing her down into the mattress,
the cloth of his jacket rough against her breasts, when
Laurel awoke suddenly and completely and froze under
him.

What was she doing, accepting the passionate love of
a man she cared nothing about? He had caught her at
a vulnerable moment, in that state between waking and
sleeping when she had been off guard. Jerking away
from the love bites nipping at her soft shoulder, she
said 'Don't!' in a voice choked with self-disgust, and
pushed against his unsuspecting bulk until she could
slide free across the bed.

'Juanita,' she gasped. 'She would never forgive us if
we—didn't taste the meal she's prepared.'

For a long time there was silence, broken only by
her own and Diego's quickened breath. It was impossible for her to bring her eyes round to witness the ebb-
ing or otherwise of passion from his face, but when he
at last spoke his voice was controlled, though having
a caustic undertone.

'Juanita understands the needs of a newly married
couple.' Straightening from the bed to a standing
position, he smoothed back the thick gloss of his hair,
then walked around the bed to stand over Laurel again.
'But perhaps you are right. Our coming together will
have the added piquancy of delay.' He bent his arm to

glance at the gold watch on his wrist. 'We can still be in time for Juanita's gastric delights if you hurry. I will save time for you by selecting a dress for you to wear.'

He went striding to the walk-in closet and re-appeared moments later with a long dress in white sculptured cotton, which he laid over the end of the bed.

'You have many beautiful dresses, *cariña*, but I will buy for you the best that Europe or New York can provide. And jewels to complement the fire and ice of your nature.'

Laurel sprang from the bed, securing the belt of her robe as she stepped past him. 'I'm not interested in clothes or jewels, *señor*. All I want is my father's release from prison.'

His hand shot out to grasp her wrist as she swept by him. 'You must know that I will do all in my power to help your father. Do you doubt that I will keep my word?'

Seeing a way out of her immediate difficulty, Laurel tugged her arm from his grip and went to the dressing table. To his reflection in the mirror, she said: 'I could believe it more easily if you guaranteed that our marriage would not be consummated until my father is free.'

From the quick rearing back of his head she knew that the proposal was a useless one.

'It could be weeks, months, before that happens. You think I am made of stone, to lie beside the wife I want and not be able to touch her?' His jaw hardened. 'No, *mi esposa*, that is not possible for me—or for you,' he stressed, and Laurel blinked, knowing he was justified in saying those words on the strength of her display a few minutes ago.

How could she have been so foolish as to respond so uninhibitedly to the touch of his mouth on an area designed by nature to be sensitive to a man's erotic stimulation? And that was all it had been, she told herself fiercely, a natural reaction of a normal woman to an attractive man—but how could she convince Diego of that? Her mouth tightened fractionally as she turned to face him.

'That's a problem that doesn't arise if we're not sharing the same bed,' she stated flatly, her composure faltering when his eyes narrowed to glittering slits and his hand possessed her wrist in a cruel grip. When he spoke, it was with the softness of a forced calm.

'Make no mistake, Laurel. Before this night is over you will belong to me as a wife belongs to her husband, willingly or not.' The hurtful grasp loosened and he let her hand fall as he turned to the door. 'I will wait for you to join me in the *sala*.'

A slow anger began to burn inside Laurel as she watched his lithe figure disappear through the door, which he closed confidently behind him. What kind of man would want a woman who so obviously didn't want him? Maybe he was the kind who got his kicks from overcoming any and all resistance to his love-making.

If so, she decided determinedly, undoing the belt of her robe and letting it slide from her shoulders to the floor, he was due for a disappointment this time. She would be as inert clay under his hands, offering no resistance but giving him no encouragement either.

Taking her under circumstances like that would be an affront to his Latin sense of *machismo*.

The decision made, Laurel felt lighter in spirit than she had since the solemn wedding service that morning as she made her way to the small *sala*.

Diego, standing with his back to her at the windows where the darkness of night pressed against the panes, saw her reflection there and turned, his breath drawing in audibly as his gaze went over the virginal white of her dress, the one he had chosen for her to wear for their wedding supper. The line was long and figure-defining, exposing the rounded tops of her breasts, and as Diego's hot gaze lingered there she wished passionately that she had not automatically succumbed to the habit of wearing whichever dress she was assigned to model. Savagely she wished, as he came quickly to lift her hand and press his lips to her palm, that she had worn her oldest jeans and sweat-shirt.

'You need no jewels to add to your beauty, *cariña*,' he murmured, the smooth olive line of his jaw hardening when she snatched her hand away.

Immediately she regretted the impulsive action, berating herself inwardly for destroying her plan of campaign right at the start.

'May I have something to drink?' she asked, seating herself in a corner of one of the deep cushioned sofas, and Diego crossed to a trolley set with an array of bottles. Without asking her preference, he poured a Martini and handed it to her silently before turning back to replenish the drink he had been holding when she came into the room.

There was a faintly mocking air in his solemnly spoken toast: 'To our long and happy marriage, my beautiful bride.' Ignoring her refusal to join him in the toast, he tossed off the measure of whisky he had poured and refilled his glass before sitting in the arm-chair he had occupied that afternoon. Laurel was relieved to see that this was evidently a drink he intended to nurture, for he laid it carelessly on the small side table by his chair.

'I assure you, *querida*,' he said drily, indicating her untouched drink with a casual hand, 'that I have not laced your Martini with some drug designed to overcome your maidenly sensitivities. I have never found it necessary to coerce a woman by those means.'

Was there a slight complacency in his veiled expression? Laurel didn't wonder that the women in his life had been many, and she could well imagine that the sexuality exuding from his every pore, not to mention his undoubted wealth and position, was sufficient to make them come running at the flick of his long, sensitive fingers. If he hadn't forced her into this marriage, she might have found him irresistible to all that was female in her nature. As it was....

She lifted the Martini and gulped it convulsively, almost choking on its strength. Diego had said that he had used no drugs, but strong liquor was equally effective as a releaser of inhibitions. And for that reason, she must be on her guard with the amount of drink she drank that evening.

'How—how soon will these people you've contacted be able to get things going on my father's case?' she asked jerkily. His frown was immediate.

'I have not yet approached them on that subject,' he said coolly.

'Not——?' Laurel stared at him aghast. 'But you promised....'

His dark head nodded in a complacent way that irritated her beyond measure. 'I promised to speak to them about your father, but my wedding day was hardly the appropriate time. In a week or two——'

'A week or two!' she repeated explosively. 'You expect my father to—to vegetate in your lousy jail while you take your own sweet time about getting him released?'

'Your father will be well taken care of,' Diego returned urbanely, picking up his glass and gazing at its contents speculatively. 'At this moment he is probably sipping on a good wine and enjoying a well cooked meal.' He gave her a sidelong glance. 'He will have all his comforts—including pleasurable company if he so desires it.'

Laurel stared at him blankly, then an awkward flush spread upward over her cheeks. 'How dare you suggest that my father would—would——'

'He is a man like any other,' Diego stated unequivocally, looking up when a tap sounded at the door and Juanita entered, her manner flustered.

In Spanish, she apologised for the lateness of the meal, but Diego waved her agitation aside. 'It is of no matter, Juanita. The Señora has not yet finished her drink.'

'*Gracias, señor*. The meal awaits your pleasure.'

Diego rose lightly to his feet as the door closed behind the housekeeper, his gaze bent significantly on Laurel's half-filled glass.

'If you will finish your drink, *querida*, we will go to the dining room. Juanita has spent many hours preparing our wedding dinner, and I would not want her to be disappointed by our tardiness.'

'Heaven forbid that Juanita should be upset in any

way,' Laurel retorted acidly, swallowing the remainder
of the Martini before getting up and stepping quickly
to the door. How ironic that Diego should display such
consideration for his servants, yet none at all as far as
her own wishes were concerned! His hand on her arm
halted her precipitate flight from the *sala*.

'Please, Laurel,' he said quietly, yet she felt the
hidden steel in his touch, 'do not in any way let Juanita
think our marriage is not one of mutual love. She has
waited many years for this day, and——'

'Bully for Juanita,' Laurel returned rudely, shaking
free of his grasp. 'Maybe she should be the one forced
to share your bed and board!' Her haughty onward
march was brought to a sudden halt in the centre of
the polished tile hall, her memory blank as to where
the dining room lay.

Tight-lipped, Diego came to take her arm and lead
her to the far side beyond the sitting room, where a
white door opened to an informal dining room, small
in comparison with the grandness of its Mexico City
counterpart. Buffets and shelves of hand-polished rose-
wood lined three of the walls, the fourth being given
over to wide windows which must overlook the cliffs
and sea during the day.

The rectangular table had been laid for two in intimate proximity at one end of the polished wood, and
the flickering light of candles was reflected on its surface.

What a waste, Laurel pondered, accepting Diego's
help in seating her. The setting, from the candles to
the floating bracts of poinsettias in a delicately curved
glass bowl, breathed of a romance most girls only
dreamed of. The man who took his place at the head
of the table to her left was also the materialisation of a

dream. The proud arrogance of his Spanish facial features was offset by the white of his dinner jacket, the deceptive smoothness of well-knit shoulders, the tapering waist and narrow hips of his ancestry were emphatically attractive. Why, then, when he must be the epitome of male desirability to so many women, did he have to pick on her for a forced marriage?

Juanita entered beaming with the first course, a thick puree of black beans seasoned with aromatic herbs and sprinkled with cheese. Laurel enjoyed the soup's tangy flavour, but scarcely tasted the tiny game hens stuffed with a seasoned wild rice mixture that followed. Diego's every glance, every gesture in her direction, spoke eloquently of his intentions when they were alone later in the matrimonial chamber. Carelessly, she imbibed more of the fine imported French wine than she had intended to.

Just as she lifted her spoon to sample the tastefully arranged dish of fresh fruits from papaya to delicate green grapes, Diego suddenly queried:

'How long were you engaged to this man in Los Angeles?'

'Brent?' Laurel stared at him. It was the first time he had broached the subject of her engagement without first having noted a certain preoccupation in her green eyes.

Lifting his glass and drinking deeply of the mellowed wine, he said drily: 'How many others have you promised yourself to, *mi esposa*?'

'Only Brent,' she returned steadily, her spoon held in abeyance. 'He was the first man I met after leaving the convent—or I should say the first man who had ever taken an interest in me as a woman. The other girls used to talk about their boy-friends, the ones they met on vacation. But I—I spent all the holidays with Dad on the boat. I didn't need anyone else.'

Diego refilled her glass in one smooth motion. 'Until this Brent came into your life.'

'Yes. He was all that my friends at school had raved about in their boy-friends.' Sensing the jealous tensing of his muscles, she pressed on relentlessly: 'In fact, more so. He's exceptionally good-looking, charming, and popular. Quite a few of the girls I knew envied me when he asked me to marry him.'

Her words ended on a choked note, but strangely it wasn't the thought of now being married to a man far removed from Brent's perfection as a partner. Memory rushed back to overwhelm her, the memory of just why she had accepted Brent's proposal.

They had come back early from a weekend spent at his parents' home in the San Fernando Valley, a weekend when Brent had increased his pressure on her to marry him. Laurel knew that his parents liked her, would be happy with the idea, but still she had held back. Part of her hesitation had been due to the unfulfilled dream of becoming a companion of the sea to her father, partly because of her indecision about a lifelong commitment to Brent. He had all the attributes her friends had described as essential, but his lovemaking had always left her vaguely dissatisfied. She had longed for him to just once forget that she had been educated in the chaste confines of a convent, to lose his head and make love to her as passionately as Diego——

What had made up her mind on that Sunday afternoon was the sight of her father's brawny arms wrapped round a buxom brunette, kissing her openly on the deck of *Dainty* before releasing her to disembark

and walk along the wooden pier to where Laurel and
Brent were approaching. Impulsively, Laurel had
turned to Brent and suggested they go to the marina
restaurant for coffee.

She hadn't wanted to meet the woman who had
probably spent the weekend with her father. Her mind
was a maelstrom of disordered thoughts as she waited
for Brent to bring the strongly brewed coffee from the
serving counter. Had she been selfish in her dreams of
being the only woman in Dan Trent's life? His liaisons
with other women would be difficult, if not impossible,
with a permanent live-aboard daughter on *Dainty*.

If Brent was surprised by her sudden decision to
accept his proposal he hid it well with his usual stoically accepting air. Brilliant academically, with him personal relationships were something that worked out or
they didn't. In the same way that he had accepted her
change of mind, he had been content to wait for
physical fulfilment until their marriage when he was
established.

Now, looking at Diego's warm eyes and sensually
triggered body, Laurel knew that he would never have
accepted such an arrangement ... or that he would
accept anything less than full consummation on his
marriage night.

'Now one of the women who envied you your
fortune,' he said harshly, reverting to their conversation, 'will be made delirious with joy at having your
cast-off lukewarm lover.'

Laurel drew a sharp breath and dropped her eyes
to the colourful fruit plate before her. The thought
of Brent with some other girl hadn't entered her mind
until now, when Diego had savagely inserted it there.

She put down her spoon and rose abruptly from the table.

'I'm tired, I want to go to be—to my room,' she amended hastily, almost bumping into Juanita who was at that moment crossing the room with a set coffee tray.

Diego was at her back immediately, his voice smooth as he told the startled housekeeper: 'The Señora is weary after the long day, Juanita. We will not require coffee.'

The dark face broke into a knowing smile. '*Si, señor. Buenas noches*,' she called to their retreating backs. 'I wish you much happiness this night.'

Laurel's fast pace went unchecked at these last words. Wherever else Diego Cesar Ramirez found his happiness this night, it wouldn't be with her!

Determinedly, she tried to close the bedroom door in his face; equally determined, he pushed it open without effort and clicked it shut with his heel.

Crossing to the elaborate dressing table, Laurel drew off her silver earrings and tossed them to its surface. 'There must be many bedrooms you can choose from in a house this size,' she bit off sharply.

'There are many,' he agreed quietly, his eyes sombre, 'but I have chosen to share this one with my wife.'

'I'm not your wife,' she snapped, kicking off her sandals and immediately regretting it when she turned to face him and found herself at a height disadvantage.

An olive hand reached out and lifted her ring hand. Reflecting accusingly up at her furious gaze was the deeply glowing emerald with its surrounding sparkle of diamonds, the duller gleam of gold from the wedding band he had placed on her finger that morning.

Snatching her hand away, she said fiercely: 'It's a

farce, and you know it. How can you expect me to be affectionate towards a man I hardly know, let alone l-love?'

Fire leaped in his eyes as he stepped closer so that their bodies almost touched. 'A good husband teaches his wife to love him in the ways that please him, *querida*,' he murmured caressingly, his hands half lifting to touch her before falling back to his sides when she spun on her heel away from him.

'You sound like something out of a Victorian melodrama, *señor*,' she threw over her shoulder. 'I may have been brought up in a convent, but I've lived all my life in a country where women have chosen independence from your kind of male chauvinism!'

'So! You prefer the lukewarm blood of the man I have rescued you from? We shall see, *chiquita*, we shall see.' Diego, a white line running from nose to mouth, went to the outer door and turned there to add menacingly: 'Be ready to receive me in ten minutes. I will wait no longer.'

Laurel stared at the door after he had gone, her brain dully registering that there must be another bedroom in the master suite if he had gone there to change. That thought was sufficient to propel her on suddenly flying feet to the big double doors. If she could lock him out, he would not risk the noise of forcible entry with Juanita no doubt still in the house clearing away their supper things.

A half sob caught in her throat when she felt for a key and found nothing but the gaping hole where one should be. Dropping to one knee, she peered through the massive keyhole and found no obstruction to her view of the outer hall. For a moment she leaned her forehead against the cool white wood of the door, then, her lips tightening resolutely, got to her feet and walked to the closet, unzipping her dress as she went, sure of only one thing when she reached for her silk dressing gown. Diego might possess her that night, but he would be taking her without enjoyment.

Unmindful of Diego's time stipulation, Laurel closed the bathroom door behind her and went about the ordinary tasks of cleaning her face of make-up and brushing her teeth. Without the cosmetic film her skin looked translucent, clear yet with an overlay of honey gold bestowed on her by the hot Mexican sun. In the direct lighting surrounding the sink area, her hair, falling to her shoulders, held a silken silver band round her head where it caught the light.

Her eyes, enormous in the beautiful bone structure of her face, reflected the deadened state of her senses. This night, her wedding night, was one she had looked forward to from girlhood with varying emotions. Most of her dreams, the romantic ones, had conjured up a faceless young husband, one who loved her so much that she would bestow her favours upon him benignly, in return expecting and receiving his undying adoration.

In her convent-induced innocence, she had not even considered in any depth the nature of the favours she would bestow. Her faceless lover would have all the gallantry of a Sir Galahad, the sensitivity of the romantic poets whose works she had devoured, the manliness of the knights who jousted for their lady's favour.

The door was thrust open suddenly, and she turned to see her husband of hours framed there, strong, dark and virile in a short brown robe of silky material which made it abundantly clear that he was as naked as the day of his birth under it. No gentle poet this!

A peculiar tightness made her voice high-pitched, like a schoolgirl's. 'I—I'm not ready.'

Without moving, his relentless gaze went over her from silver hair to pink toes peeping from under the white silk of her robe. In turn, her eyes shifted nervously over the deep vee exposed where his robe had been carelessly tied to reveal a smooth-skinned olive chest, and down to the sinewy length of male leg and long feet.

Her breath drew in on a frightened gasp and she turned blindly to tidy away the evidence of her toilette.

'Leave that,' he commanded tersely. 'Leave it and come to me.'

Her fingers froze on the toothpaste tube, its slashing red and white colours imprinted indelibly on her mind. Then, as if his voice was that of her hypnotic master, she went to him fatalistically, as if her whole life had led up to this moment when a pagan stranger would take her in his arms, bruising her soft lips with the hungry abrasion of his, bending the slender line of her body to the demanding arch of his, making her head swim with the blatant force of his masculinity.

Only the touch of his warmth on her flesh told her that her robe had been discarded, that he had lifted her against his smoothly muscled chest and was carrying her to the bedroom, his mouth hot at her ear pouring out words of Spanish which she was too disorientated to translate.

He laid her gently on the yielding bed, joining her there, his body flesh warm over the cool shrinking of hers. His mouth seemed to be everywhere at once ... at her throat, her closed lids, the soft line of her cheek, stealing her breath when it finally closed possessively over her trembling lips.

Her determination to stay cool and ungiving was swept away in the practised assault he made on her senses. His needs suddenly and urgently became her needs, his desire to possess her desire to yield.

'*Amorcita*,' he murmured feverishly when her hands ran with a possession of their own across the smooth gold of his shoulders and down the length of his spine, coming back by the same route to mesh her fingers in the thickness of his black hair. '*Te adoro.*'

Her voice murmured too in her own language, words she had no recollection of until Diego's lithe warmth stiffened above her and she heard the lingering echo of her own 'Oh Brent—darling!'

Then Diego's fingers entwined themselves in her hair, pulling it back painfully from her scalp.

'What did you say?' he demanded hoarsely, sending a shiver across her heated skin. A shiver that seemed to clear her brain suddenly and make mockery of the golden body pressing hers into the mattress. Here was the perfect solution, the one she had racked her brains to find!

'Did I say something?' she asked in a breathy whisper.

'You said the name of Brent,' he accused, black eyes staring hard into the darkened green of hers.

'Oh.' A small frown creased the smooth area between her brows. 'Well, that's not surprising in this kind of situation, is it? After all, Brent and I were ...' She allowed her voice to trail off delicately, and felt the tremor of anger that rippled through the taut body pinning hers.

'He was your lover?' Diego questioned with awful quietness.

Laurel's green eyes met his with purposeful blank-

ness. 'What do you think?' A throaty laugh bubbled
from her lips, the sound tightening his smooth jaw to
steel. 'An engaged couple in America has much more
freedom than in your country, *señor*. Did you really
think Brent and I would consider marriage without
finding out if we were suited in every way?'

Diego shifted so that his weight was blessedly lifted
from her rapidly numbing limbs, but the wild glint in
his eyes pinned her just as effectively to the mattress.

'I cannot take as my wife a woman who has been—
used by another man,' he bit off tersely, his clasp
tightening painfully on her hair. 'You knew this about
me, yet you married me. Why?'

Laurel managed a shrug, although her scalp pained
sharply where he tugged at her hair. 'You gave me little
choice, *señor*. My father——'

Diego uttered a string of oaths in Spanish and sprang
from the bed, mercifully releasing his hold on her hair,
and after he had shrugged into the robe he had cast
aside, he turned to look coldly down at her.

'You expect me to help your father after *this*?' he
threw down caustically. 'Think again, Laurel! Your
father can stay in prison and rot, as you called it, as
far as I am concerned!'

Laurel stared numbly after him as he strode from the
bed, ignoring her state of nudity for long minutes after
the door had closed behind him. She had saved her
precious virginity, but what had she done to her father?

CHAPTER SEVEN

'LAUREL!'

Reluctantly, Laurel forced her heavy lids half open and stared dazedly at a pair of male legs clad in immaculate cream slacks beside the bed. For a moment panic gripped her as she wondered where she was, and fear widened her eyes as they travelled up past the legs to brown knit shirt stretched tautly over smoothly contoured chest muscles. The face above was darkly brooding, the haughtily aristocratic features the ones which had haunted the light sleep she had fallen into just before dawn.

Diego indicated with one light brown hand the tray that had been placed upon the bedside table.

'I have brought your breakfast. Juanita would have found it strange that——' His eyes flickered over the unruffled half of the wide bed.

His gaze returned contemptuously to her, and through his eyes she saw her own sleepily awakened state, hair spilling over the pillows in a spread of pure silver. Her limbs seemed incapable of movement as she stared up at the cold surface of his eyes.

'Wh-what did you tell her?'

'What do you think I told her?' Swinging away from her, he went to the windows and pulled the full-length curtains aside, letting in a flood of light that made Laurel put a protective hand to her eyes. 'That I found my wife impure and spent the night apart from her?'

The words were spoken with such a lack of the savagery Laurel had expected that she felt the unaccustomed prickle of tears behind her eyes. There was something so pathetically vulnerable about the proud stance of his virile male body, hands thrust into slacks pockets as he gazed from the window, that she wanted to cry out a denial. A denial that Brent had ever done more than titillate the strong sensual streak she now knew ran deeply, shockingly, through her. And that it had been Diego who had roused that sleeping tiger in her. Most of the reason for her sleeplessness had been because her body, like a separate entity from her mind, had been reacting to the abrupt cessation of his expert lovemaking the night before.

Struggling to a sitting position, tonguetied in face of his silence, Laurel glanced at the tray beside her. The tempting aroma of freshly baked rolls coming from the basket where they lay wrapped in stiff white linen mingled with the odour of coffee from the silver pot. Golden curls of butter filled a small dish, but it was the silver bud vase that drew her attention with its single half-opened rose of clear orange red. Its vibrant colour seemed to hold all the warmth and vitality of the land from which it had drawn succour, and Laurel swallowed the awkward lump that had risen to her throat.

'Th-thank you for the tray,' she murmured as Diego turned from the window and stepped towards the bed, freeing his hands from his pockets. 'The rose is— beautiful.'

The shrug of his shoulders was eloquent. 'The tray was not of my doing. You have Juanita to thank for it.'

'Oh.'

Illogical disappointment surged through her, a state which was not alleviated when Diego drew a small box from his pocket and tossed it on to the bed beside her.

'You might as well have this gift, too. It is a custom for the bride to receive a token of her husband's appreciation for her abundant favours bestowed on the wedding night.' His mouth twisted into a sarcastic line as Laurel stared at the green jeweller's box. 'Open it. I will expect you to wear them at dinner tonight.'

Laurel obeyed his imperative command, her slender fingers shaking as they picked up the box and pressed the catch to open it. Inside lay a pair of exquisitely designed earrings, emeralds surrounded by diamonds to match her engagement ring.

'They're—beautiful,' she managed, her mouth firming when her eyes met the bleakness in his. 'But you should keep them for your wife.'

'You are my wife. I have told you, I will marry only once in my lifetime.'

Her eyes widened as the import of his words sank in. Then, her voice a whisper, she said: 'You want to stay married to *me*, after last night?' She laughed suddenly, mirthlessly. 'You're no monk, *señor*! I can't see you living the celibate life somehow.'

One arrogant black brow arched up. 'I said nothing of living a monk's life, *mi esposa*! Until my distaste for soiled merchandise dissipates, there are other women who can care for my needs.'

Laurel gasped as if he had struck her, then said bitterly: 'And they're not soiled, as you call it by your double standard?'

'I have never elevated one of them to be my wife,' he returned evenly, turning on his heel to go to the door. 'Have your breakfast. We will swim in the pool before lunch, and after a rest this afternoon we will visit with your father.'

With these dogmatic words he went from the room, leaving Laurel seething at his high-handed doling out of orders with no expectation of dissent.

Her mouth dry, she poured coffee from the silver pot into the delicate china cup and sipped avidly on its lukewarm comfort. She was no better off than she had been the night before, the only difference being that now she was forced into a game of cat and mouse, with Diego as predator and herself as unwilling victim. At any time, when he tired of the women ready to oblige him, he would pounce on her and make her his wife in every sense of the word. And he would know that she had lied to him.

But at least he seemed to have reversed his decision to do nothing to help her father, and that was the lifeline she must hold to.

The morning was well advanced when she went hesitantly into the main part of the house and met a shyly beaming Juanita crossing the hall. An unwitting blush bathed her cheeks when she realised what the housekeeper must be thinking, and the blush seemed to confirm the Mexican woman's surmise of a night spent in the arms of her virile husband.

'*Buenos dias, señora,*' the dark-skinned woman said softly, her eyes darting quickly from Laurel's severely bound hair to her long shapely legs under green floral beach jacket.

'*Buenos dias,* Juanita.' The woman seemed delighted when she asked in Spanish where the Señor was to be found, and replied in a rapid spate that Diego was already swimming in the pool. 'I will bring refreshments there if you would like them, *señora*.'

'*Gracias.* Just some hot coffee if you have it.'

'I will bring it at once.'

Laurel, relying on her hazily remembered sense of direction, went with what she hoped was confidence to the side patio doors, opening one and stepping out on to the coolness of a tiled patio where tubbed greenery flourished despite the wide overhang of the house. Beyond it, the pool sparkled in deep turquoise under a sun that blazed from a perfectly blue sky.

She had an opportunity to study the olive-toned figure poised on the diving board at one end of the rectangular pool, and despite herself her heart quickened to an erratic beat as she surveyed the long lines of masculine perfection. Blue-black hair glistened in the sun above shoulders moulded in light bronze and muscled chest smoothly hairless leading to flat stomach and hard male thighs tapering to well-formed calves and feet.

As she watched, unnoticed, Diego raised his arms in a reverentially pagan way, reminiscent of the divers off La Quebrada cliffs in Acapulco, then did a quick jack-knife dive into the pool, his body leaving a wake of froth when he surfaced and swam vigorously to the far end.

By the time he had swum back the length of the pool's glittering surface, Laurel was ensconced on one of the padded loungers facing the sun, smoothing lotion on the honey-gold skin of her long legs.

Every sense on the alert, she was aware of his dripping body coming to stand at the foot of her chair, but kept her eyes on the motion of her hand as it smoothed the cream deep into her skin.

At last Diego said drily: 'With so much rubbing, *querida*, even our hot Mexican sun would hesitate to penetrate beyond the surface of your skin.'

While she was still wondering if the words had a

hidden, snide meaning, Diego took the bottle of lotion from her hand and indicated her shoulders.

'If you will permit?' he asked, and without waiting for an answer he poured some of the lotion into his hands and began a slow massaging movement over her shoulders, ignoring her initial shrug of rejection and her irritable: 'I can do it myself!'

But she had to admit, as the supple hands unknotted the lump of tension at her nape, that his touch was far superior to her own. Not, she thought drowsily, that soothing massage was what she had had in mind, but her every sinew ached with the strain of the past twenty-four hours. Added to that was the loss of sleep during the long night, and her lids had already closed when she felt the soothing hands slide with oiled smoothness under the brief covering at her breasts, a male mouth nibbling warmly at her ear.

She stiffened immediately, pushing away the languor that had invaded her limbs and jerking upright on the thick cushions. At the sound of Juanita's apologetic: '*Perdon, señor*. The Señora's coffee ...' her head whipped round and embarrassment sent guilty colour up over her skin. The housekeeper must have seen Diego's intimate touch under the white swimsuit, the mouth which seemed to have been uttering passionate phrases at her ear. Indeed, the older woman's smile held more than a hint of coy delight as Diego murmured his thanks.

'How dare you?' Laurel hissed as the plump figure in floral cotton housedress retreated towards the house. 'She must have thought——'

'That we wish to prolong the sweetness of the night hours in each other's arms?' he finished coolly, giving his inimical light shrug as he came round to sit at the bottom of her lounger and pour coffee from the tray Juanita had set down on a patio table next to it. 'She has already reported to her husband the success of our coming together, interpreting the shadows under your eyes to mean that I gave my bride little rest.'

With the sun blazing behind him, his expression was difficult to read, but Laurel raised her hand automatically to accept the delicately shaped china cup from him. He had wanted Juanita to think . . .

'Is the opinion of servants so important to you?' she mocked, wanting to hurt him as her tormented nerves had been brought to screaming pitch.

She saw the proud tilt of his head as he turned it slowly, levelling his gaze on her. '*Si*, it is important to me on this matter. When I came here to vacation as a boy, Carlos and Juanita were the only parents I knew. They have waited long for my marriage, and the prospect of caring for my children, and I will not disappoint them.'

Laurel leaned back against the hot cushion so quickly that a small amount of coffee spilled into her saucer. Diego was at once attentive, taking it from her and cleaning it with a paper napkin before handing it back.

'Be very careful, *querida*,' he warned softly, and Laurel sensed that his meaning was far from coffee spills.

'What's to stop me from telling them that our marriage is no real marriage?'

His teeth glinted whitely against his dark skin. 'For one thing, they would not believe you. And for another, I would very quickly establish the reality of our marriage.'

'Really?' she stabbed waspishly. 'And what would your saintly mother have said about that?' She had had

no intention of ever letting him know that in an odd
way Consuelo's shrewish insinuation regarding her likeness to Diego's mother had any power to hurt her. Now
his eyes had narrowed to glittering slits, and she took
a hasty gulp of the hot coffee.

'Who has been speaking of my mother to you?' he
demanded grittily.

'I—I saw her portrait in the Mexico City house. It
would have been hard to miss the likeness between her
and myself.'

His hard gaze went calculatingly over her pale hair
and femininely curved body with its long length of leg,
then he gave a dismissing shrug. 'There is a slight surface resemblance but there can be no real comparison
between you.'

Of course not, Laurel mocked inwardly. How could
any woman be compared to the Madonna-like purity of
his dead mother?

Diego rose abruptly from the lounger and looked
down at her, his face seemingly moulded from hard
bronze. 'I am going to swim again before lunch. Will
you join me?'

When Laurel shook her head he turned and strode
off to the pool, droplets of water raining on her heated
skin when he dived neatly from the side. He seemed as
supremely confident in the pool as on land, his dark
gold limbs cleaving through the smooth surface water
with a graceful economy of movement.

Perhaps she should have swum in the pool. The sun
burned in a red haze through her closed lids and
lethargy crept over her, relaxing her body while her
mind remained active. On second thoughts, maybe it
was as well she hadn't joined Diego in the water. They
would inevitably have touched at some point or other,

and she was at odds with herself as to whether that would be a good thing at this stage in their odd relationship.

Etched behind her lids now was an involuntary picture of his hard, warm body making love to her in the wide matrimonial bed, and her own shattering response to a man she had thought she hated and feared. Still hated, she reminded herself, though now her fear was more concerned with her own physical reactions than with Diego's ability to hurt her.

As soon as her father was freed she would be leaving the marriage Diego had forced on her, leaving this tumultuous country where passions ran high and resistance melted in the steamy heat of the ever-present sun. An annulment should be easier to obtain in her own country—without Diego's agreement, it would be almost impossible here, where his influence was so strong.

Yet, as consciousness slowly receded to the same sound that had eventually sent her off into sleep that dawn, the rhythmic ebb and flow of the sea, she felt again Diego's smoothly intimate touch for Juanita's benefit, and a heat that had little to do with the sun seared the length of her body.

Diego drew the sleek grey Mercedes to a halt almost opposite the police station and glanced cynically at the white-knuckled hands Laurel clasped on the lap of her lime green silk dress. The matching green of her eyes was obscured by dark-lensed sunglasses, and her thoughts ran riot behind their screening mask.

'You bear the looks of an outraged spinster, *cariña*, not the blushing radiance of a bride who has lain in her husband's arms on their wedding night.' His voice was softly mocking, his expressive mouth carved slightly into a sardonic smile, and Laurel turned on him to vent the pent-up fury she had barely been able to control during the drive into Acapulco from Jacintha Point.

'Do you think my father will be fooled anyway by this ridiculous excuse for a marriage?' she flared, adding deliberately: 'He and my mother loved each other from the minute they laid eyes on each other. Don't you think he knows the way two people in love look, especially after their—their——'

'Their first lovemaking?' Diego inserted coolly. 'But then, *mi mujer*, doubtless your mother did not come to his bed from another man's.' Laurel's outraged gasp was cut short when his arm circled her shoulders and drew her to him, his other hand removing the sunglasses from her indignant eyes. 'However, if you wish to present the picture of a well-loved wife, that is easily accomplished.'

His hand cupped her chin, forcing it not ungently upward until her eyes glared greenly into his. Then, unmindful of the interested looks of two patrolmen about to enter the police station, he bent his head and took hard possession of her lips, kissing her insistently until her mouth parted under his masterful pressure. Resenting his possessive claim, and the swift surge of her own pulses, Laurel brought her hand up to tug at his hair in an effort to free herself, but she had done no more than grasp a handful of the blue-black growth when her attention was diverted to the sensation of her own hair being freed from its confining pins.

Then she forgot everything in her struggle to maintain a balance that steadily became more weighted in favour of the sensations sweeping her. The sweet rob-

bery of Diego's plundering mouth, the supple fingers
that combed through her hair, then held firmly to her
head in an unnecessary manoeuvre to keep her mouth
in the position he wanted, combined to send her senses
swirling into a vortex of passionate desire. A desire she
had never known before, yet part of her had always
known of its existence, that some day a man would
come to light its flame within her. Shocked, she realised
as Diego murmured against her lips that Brent could
never have been that counterpart to her own sexuality.

'Diego?' she whispered wonderingly at his ear, his
mouth pressed now to the tender join of shoulder and
neck, and felt shock jolt through her when he stiffened
momentarily, then thrust her away from him abruptly.
The hot liquid of his eyes surveyed her dishevelled
appearance, and she was conscious all at once of her disordered hair, flushed cheeks, mouth swollen with the
imprint of his lips.

'So,' he observed with satisfaction, only a slight huskiness betraying his own arousal, 'you now look well
loved. Even your father will not doubt its truth. No,'
he commanded sharply as Laurel drew a shuddering
breath and searched feverishly in her bag for a comb
and lipstick, 'make no repairs—or we will have to go
through the process again.'

'And you wouldn't want that, would you?' she threw
at him across the space of the car, humiliation smarting
like prickly heat on her skin.

'No, I would not,' he agreed quietly, opening his
door and smoothing his ruffled hair as he came round
the front of the car to open her door, evidently not
seeing, or ignoring, the grinning policemen who at last
turned into the station.

When she reached for her sunglasses on the dashboard, Diego's hand came out to capture her wrist. 'Leave them there, *niña*, your eyes reveal the required sparkle of—knowledge.'

Laurel felt the touch of his hand on her arm as a fiery brand, yet she was glad of his nearness when they entered the dismal building and were greeted by the same officer she had seen on her first visit to the prison. An obsequious officer now as he came from behind his desk to greet Diego, but the other two men eyed her with such obvious lewdness that she instinctively pressed her side to Diego's and felt his arm reach instantly round her waist. He kept it there as they followed the duty officer along the dank corridor to her father's cell. But as soon as he had opened the door with a flourish of keys, she broke from Diego's hold and rushed into the room, halting at the rough table suddenly, her eyes seeking her father's tall form stretched on the cot. Only now it wasn't a rough cot, it was a real bed complete with mattresses and coloured blankets.

'Dad! It's me, Laurel!'

Dan turned his face from the wall, and he blinked as if waking from a deep sleep. 'Laurel? Is it really you?' With what seemed an almighty effort, he pushed his legs over the side of the bed and in another moment was standing holding her in his arms. 'I thought I was still dreaming. Sorry, honey, I guess I didn't expect to see you this soon after your wedding. I'd have cleaned up a bit if I'd known you were coming.'

Her head buried on his chest, Laurel felt his arm reach behind her.

'Diego? Congratulations.' His hands came then to Laurel's shoulders, putting her away from him so that he could look into her eyes. Her mouth trembled at the greyness in his face, but his smile was unforced when he said softly: 'Yes, I can see the wedding went off all right. I've never seen you look the way you do right now, honey, and you don't know how happy that makes me.'

'I just wished,' she choked, 'that you could have been there too. I—I had nobody.'

Dan's hands tightened on her shoulders, though he was silent for a few moments. At last he said huskily: 'You had your husband, Laurel, and that's more important than having any number of relatives and friends around you.'

She stifled a sob as she turned involuntarily to look at Diego, surprising a glimmer of compassion, tenderness, in the dark intentness of his eyes as he watched father and daughter.

'I—yes, I have Diego,' she said flatly, knowing that her husband possessed all the smooth suavity of his race and could summon up appropriate expressions on demand.

'Well, let's sit down and talk for a while, though I know you two want to get back to being alone ... and this isn't exactly the Hilton,' Dan's eyes went wryly round the small room as he waved them to the padded leather chairs surounding the table. These, too, were an extra embellishment since Laurel's last visit, and her eyes swept quickly round the walls, discovering a wardrobe whose half-open doors revealed a goodly selection of her father's clothes, and next to that a small table well stocked with liquor bottles and glasses. Her mouth tightened on a tremor. It had been obvious from the odour on Dan's breath that he had already imbibed freely that afternoon from his abundant supply.

'I want to thank you, Diego, for all you've done to

make the place a bit more livable,' he said now with what Laurel felt was forced geniality. 'In fact, a lot more—I can even offer you a drink to celebrate the nuptials. Laurel?'

It was on the tip of Laurel's tongue to refuse the drink, but a forceful glance from Diego made her say chokily: 'I'll—have rum and coke.'

Diego chose whisky and her father poured a generous measure of five-star brandy for himself. Holding up his own glass after handing Diego his, he proposed a toast to their happiness. Looking at Laurel, he said emotionally:

'May your marriage be as perfect as your mother's and mine was.'

Laurel's throat closed as she sipped her drink, making her cough and choke slightly. Face red, she looked over and caught the sardonic glitter in Diego's eyes.

'A record like that would be hard to beat, Dad,' she gasped, her eyes filled with tears which could have been caused by the misdirection of the rum, but she knew it was not. Never in her wildest imaginings would she have envisioned her father's toast to her wedding being given in a Mexican jail cell with her husband of hours glinting his contempt for her over the rim of his glass. No, her dreams had been more along the lines of being borne down the aisle on her father's arm, and of being given by him in marriage to—Brent. Already she was finding it difficult to recall Brent's face in detail; instead, the haughtily aristocratic features of Diego Ramirez were superimposed on her brain. The tautening at the pit of her stomach told her she was still responding to the calculated passion he had inspired in the car before entering the jail, and it was several minutes before she came to with a start and realised that her father and Diego had been holding a conversation, and that Diego was addressing Dan familiarly as 'My friend.'

She gazed curiously at her father, who had remained standing, realising with irritation that the two men did indeed appear to be on a friendly basis—their link in common being herself, she thought sadly. If only she could confide in her father, or even spend just a few minutes alone with him. Loneliness in a family sense she had lived with for a long time, but at least Dan had always been there in vacation time to listen to her hurts and woes. Now she was more scared, more out of her depth than she had ever been, but the last person she could confide in was her father.

As if sensing her disturbance, Diego stood up and placed his glass on the table. 'We must go now, *querida*,' he said gently, then turned to Dan. 'My housekeeper is hopeful that the meal she prepares tonight will be appreciated more than last night's, *amigo*.'

To Laurel's horror, her father gave an understanding man-to-man chuckle of understanding and assured Diego that tonight would be different.

'The wedding night can be the worst in the whole marriage,' he added knowledgeably, and Laurel's lips were cool on his cheek as she wished him goodnight. Diego had walked tactfully to the door, and Dan said huskily:

'You have a good man there, honey, take care of each other. That's what your mother and I did, and I don't believe either of us regretted anything for a minute.'

Laurel wanted to cry out that already she was regretting marrying a man she didn't love, could never love in the way that her mother had loved Dan. Instead, as she drew away she asked huskily: 'You like him, don't you?'

'Yes, I do.' His blue eyes looked searchingly into hers. 'He'll be good to you, honey, I knew that from the first time I saw him look at you at the El Mirador. And that's not to say,' he smiled, lifting her chin so that her eyes met his, 'that I don't think he's the luckiest guy in the world. I've told him so, and he agreed.'

'Did he now?' Laurel asked, unconsciously bitter.

Dan's fingers tightened on her chin. 'Laurel, you're happy with him? Now that you've—well, been with him? Wedding nights can be traumatic, so don't judge your entire future by that.'

Realising she had been selfishly eliciting his sympathy in a roundabout way, she drew a shaky breath and smiled tremulously. 'Yes, I'm—happy, Dad. As I said before, my whole future is tied up in Diego.'

He seemed satisfied with that, but as Laurel joined Diego at the door she had to blink rapidly to disperse the tears threatening to drown her eyes, and was hardly aware of Diego's firm hand at her waist urging her forward.

'Are you all right?' he asked when they were seated in the car, Laurel dabbing at her eyes and staring stoically from the side window.

'Of course I'm not all right!' she snapped fiercely, a sob in her voice. 'How do you expect me to feel? I'm married to a man I hate the sight of, and my father is shut up in—in *there*!' She gestured wildly towards the unprepossessing lines of the jail opposite, her eyes following her arm and stopping when they reached the tense line of Diego's jaw. His eyes had suddenly become bleak, in direct contrast to their normal

warmth, but he said nothing as he started the car and
set it in motion.

No word was passed between them as he drove fast
and furiously back to Jacintha Point. Once or twice
Laurel slanted a sideways look at him, and always his
profile had a dark sullen look that sent shivers skitter-
ing over her spine. He had been angry last night, but
this was something else again, something that had gone
beyond anger into a realm she knew nothing of.

A sense of fatalism overtook her as he hustled her
into the house, ignoring Juanita's startled round eyes
in the hall on his relentless drive into the master suite.
By the time they reached the comfortably furnished
bedroom, Laurel was convinced that he had decided
to extract revenge for her assertion of hate for him in
the only way such a man would envisage. Strangely, the
prospect of being taken forcibly now left her unmoved.
All she wanted was for it to be over with, for the deadly
coldness to lift from Diego's features, made to express
warmth and vitality.

'Diego,' she whispered when he let her go, almost
throwing her from him. Dimly she knew that bruises
would appear where his fingers had dug into the soft
flesh of her arm, but that wasn't important as she faced
him and faltered again: 'Diego?'

'Sit down!' he ordered harshly, repeating the words
in a louder pitch when she took a pleading step towards
him. 'Sit down and listen to what I have to say.'

She sank into one of the tub chairs arranged to take
advantage of the sea vista, her eyes never leaving the
tense set of his face. But it was several minutes before
he spoke from the window where he had gone to stand
with his back to her. His long-fingered hands were
clenched into fists at his sides, but his head had its

usual arrogantly proud lift.

'I was wrong,' he said in a voice that was controlled yet held a note of unevenness. 'Wrong to marry you and take you from the man who is your husband in all but name. Wrong to take advantage of your father's predicament to force you into a marriage with a man you could do nothing but hate. I thought I could force you into loving me in the same way, but——' He shrugged eloquently and turned his dark head to meet her eyes.

'Love—can't be forced,' Laurel said shakily.

'I know that now. That is why——' his eyes went unseeingly to the marine panorama outside the window, 'I will expect nothing from you. It is best that you remain my wife for some time. It is true that I can do more for your father in that way, but when he is released, you too may have your freedom.'

'You mean——?'

'An annulment, yes,' he nodded, turning from the window to stride to the door, shoulders a stiffly held line under the grey jacket of his suit.

'But, Diego——'

'This is what you wanted, is it not?' he turned on her savagely. 'To free your father and go back to the man you love?'

The sharp pain in her chest made Laurel's 'Yes!' sound more vehement than she had intended, and she watched numbly as Diego wheeled on his heel and went from the room.

CHAPTER EIGHT

'YOUR husband is indeed fortunate to have found such a flower to grace his table, Señora Ramirez,' the man at Laurel's right flattered extravagantly.

Her eyes went to the top of the extended table where Diego's dark head was bent attentively to listen to what the attractive woman to his right was saying. It was hard to tell from this distance, of course, but his eyes seemed to glitter his male appreciation for the woman's darkly flamboyant beauty shown to advantage in a white figure-hugging dress which left smooth olive shoulders bare and revealed a tantalising glimpse of maturely rounded breasts.

'I doubt if my husband has ever experienced much trouble in finding flowers to decorate his table, *señor*,' Laurel smiled tightly to mask the tartness of her reply, but the distinguished-looking older man beside her cast a shrewd look in the direction her eyes had taken.

'Have no fears where Francisca is concerned, *señora*,' he said softly. 'What was between her and your husband was over a long time ago. She married elsewhere, and I understand she was happy with her husband.'

'Was?'

'Regrettably, Anton died recently. Because it was his country, they lived in France. Now Francisca has returned to her homeland where she has many friends to help her adjust to her loss.' He gave the inevitable Latin shrug which expressed so much in one movement.

Diego's hand reached over to cover Francisca's lying idly on the table between them, and was still there several moments later when Laurel returned her attention to the crème caramel dessert before her. Her appetite gone, she laid her spoon beside the dish and signalled unobtrusively to the major domo who presided over the side buffets. Moments later, coffee and liqueurs were being served to the twenty guests, and Laurel had time to glance down the table to where Diego was now speaking with courteously bent head to the couple on his left.

This was the third such dinner party they had given since their return from Acapulco, and already she was becoming used to the idea of presiding over a table at which were seated some of Mexico's most prominent citizens. Overruling her earlier qualms, Diego had informed her coolly that such social occasions were necessary to his efforts of setting the wheels in motion for Dan's trial and release.

'In my country, these matters cannot be rushed,' he had told her one morning at the breakfast they usually shared before he left for his office. 'We will entertain two, or perhaps three times before inviting the people important to our cause.'

'And while you play this slow dance of unfoldment,' Laurel had snapped shrewishly, 'my father is——'

'Your father is as comfortable as possible in the circumstances,' Diego had gritted, pushing his chair back with an angry movement and towering over her as she sat at the other side of the intimate round table.

'He gets no fresh air,' Laurel had returned sullenly. 'His face is positively grey from lack of sunshine.'

'I am sorry I was not able to arrange for him to be

taken to the beach each day to sun himself,' was Diego's sarcastic response, and he had taken himself off before Laurel had time to make even a token apology.

An apology he was due. Without Diego's help, her father would have been in much direr straits than he now was. She knew that, yet some demon she had been unaware of possessing always urged her on to provoke this man who was her husband in fact but not in deed. Perhaps it was a streak of feminine pique at his calm acceptance of the status quo between them. For all the attention he had paid to her as a woman since the night at Jacintha Point when he had told her she would have her freedom, she could have been a marble statue he had bought for his collection.

And it was as an inanimate object that he had admired her during those interminable days of their pseudo-honeymoon. With every change of clothes, from brief sundresses to swimsuits to elegant evening wear, she had been aware of his appreciation of her slender beauty, but knew at the same time that it was admiration from afar. While her own pulses raced treacherously at his slightest touch, intended or inadvertent, his features remained impassively closed.

Which was something, she told herself wryly, for a man of his temperament whose emotions of the moment were usually highly readable. She had never had doubts about the desire he had felt for her on the few occasions when she had been in his arms. The memory of their wedding night, when they had come so close to consummating the marriage he had forced, still haunted her restless nights in the postered matrimonial bed upstairs....

'Sorry?' she blinked to the older man at her right,

realising suddenly that he had been addressing her not for the first time. 'I must have been dreaming,' she laughed awkwardly.

'Your husband is a very lucky man,' he said again, a twinkle lighting the darkness of eyes set in a fine network of aged lines, 'to be able to inspire such dreams in his bride on an occasion such as this. I think Diego has been trying to attract your attention for some time —perhaps to signal to you that dinner is over?' he added tactfully.

'Oh. Yes.' Flustered, her eyes met the forbidding black of Diego's down the length of the table, and for a moment it was as if she were paralysed in her seat. Then, still amazed that people engrossed in laughing conversation one minute would immediately take her cue, she led the way into the formal salon. There she took up a stance before the baroque fireplace and watched as the guests gravitated to different areas of the huge, high-ceilinged room.

This was the night, she had no need to remind herself, when the Justice Minister and two of his aides were in attendance. The night when Diego would take his first step towards effecting her father's release. Would he speak to them at the now empty dining table, or take them into the comfortably furnished study off the main hall?

Her attention was diverted by the small talk of people wanting to thank her for the stupendous meal she had provided.

'I did no more than agree to the menu the chef sent to me,' she admitted honestly with a smile. 'And Diego's staff are so well trained that it needs only a minimal effort on my part.'

Her stomach turned and dropped when her roving

eye caught sight of the Justice Minister listening intently to something one of his aides was telling him.
The other assistant was at the far side of the room,
chatting with the older couple who had been sitting
on Diego's left at the table.

Where was Diego?

With a murmured apology, and noting that black-
clad servants were circulating with trays of additional
refreshments, Laurel made her way unobtrusively to
the double doors thrown wide for the occasion. A
glimpse into the dining room where maids were busily
clearing the table made it clear that Diego hadn't
lingered there, and she swivelled thoughtfully on the
heel of her sandal. Could he have gone to the study to
be alone for a while? It wasn't like him to shut himself
away from their guests, but perhaps there had been a
phone call. It seemed to ring incessantly for him when
he was at home, even in Acapulco, but this one seemed
to be taking an interminable time.

Crossing the hall past the soothing splash of the
fountain, its pool strewn with camellia blossoms for the
occasion, she went across the tiled floor to the recessed
study door. Pausing there for a moment with her ear
to it before realising that no sound would penetrate its
solid thickness, she turned the black iron handle and
went in.

Diego was just lifting his head from the tear-stained
face of the woman he held in his arms. Francisca.

Diego was the first to recover himself. His expression,
which had hardened at the sight of Laurel, softened
again as he looked down into Francisca's mortified eyes.

'Go now, *cara,*' he husked softly. 'We will talk again
later.'

Released from his arms, Francisca hurried past Laurel with downcast eyes. Diego took a slender cigar from the humidor on his desk and lit it with steady fingers before turning to look fully at Laurel, his features set again into the controlled pattern she had become used to.

'So, *mi esposa*,' his voice came mockingly as smoke curled up past his glittering black eyes, 'you have a reason for tracking me to my lair?'

The icy shock Laurel had experienced on seeing Francisca wrapped in his arms thawed in the sudden heat of her anger.

'I don't care how many women you make love to in this room,' she lashed, scarcely recognising the high-pitched voice as her own, 'or even that you are neglecting guests you have asked to your house. All I'm concerned with is that you're breaking your promise to speak to the men who can get my father out of your lousy jail!'

The hard line of Diego's jaw tautened to granite, but he took his time about answering her, first flicking the ash from his cigar into the ashtray on the desk, then going to lower himself into the black leather chair behind it.

'I have broken no promises,' he observed evenly, studying the dull glow at the end of the cigar. 'There was never any intention on my part to speak of your father to them tonight.'

'But you told me——'

'I told you that these matters must be undertaken slowly in my country,' his voice rose dangerously. 'It would not be correct for me to approach these men when they are guests in my home.'

Laurel made a rush for the desk and banged her

closed fist on its leather surface. 'I don't give a damn for your snail's pace courtesy,' she railed, her voice verging on hysteria, then she pivoted on her heel. 'If you won't talk to them, then I will!'

Her fingers had barely touched the heavy door handle when Diego caught up to her and swung her round to face him, his fingers like pincers on her wrist.

'You will not embarrass guests in my home!' he ground out, his face white under the tan. 'Go to your room now, and I will apologise for your absence. I will speak with you later.'

'Before or after you speak with Francisca?' she jeered. 'You're having quite a night with your women, aren't you?'

Releasing her wrist, he took a step back from her and said quietly: 'I owe you no loyalty in that connection.'

'Then you can't stop me from going out there,' she challenged, chin high as she glared at him, her heart tripping in sudden fright when he leaned forward to jerk the heavy doors open, then stooped to lift her effortlessly into his arms.

'In that you are mistaken, *mujer regañonna*,' he pronounced grimly, and proceeded to carry her past the pattering fountain to the broad sweep of red-carpeted stairs leading to the upper floor.

'Shrew wife, am I?' she panted, and struck out at his face with her free hand, hearing only dimly the hum of voices from the salon. 'You haven't seen anything yet!'

'*Por Dios*, you try me too far!' Diego swore explosively, pausing only momentarily to twist her arm cruelly behind her back and so leave her impotent as he continued his progress up the stairs.

Laurel lay quiescent in his arms, partly because he had disarmed her, but mostly because of her sudden tumultuous awareness of his nearness, of the soft strain of her breasts against the hard warmth of male chest under white dinner jacket, the musky scent of the cologne he used drifting towards her nostrils making her dizzy.

Inside the bedroom his steps were soundless as he walked to the bed already drawn back and dropped Laurel on its yielding surface, his breath coming only slightly more rapidly from the exertion of carrying her up the long flight of stairs.

'You will stay here until I have seen to our guests. They will be leaving soon, and then we will talk.'

Struggling with the unbelievable sensations coursing through her, Laurel could only gaze up helplessly into the hard glitter of his eyes, her tongue locked in the dryness of her mouth. For another moment Diego stood over her, looking broodingly down into the green eyes widened in stunned recognition. Just before he turned away, the harsh lines of his mouth appeared to soften, but there was no lessening of the dark fury in his eyes.

Laurel watched his swift retreat to the door, his hand reaching for the heavy key in the door lock, and heard the sound of its insertion and turning on the outside. Still she lay as if paralysed, staring at the door he had gone through. Then, slowly, her hand came up to cover her eyes as if in that way she could shut out the knowledge she didn't want to—couldn't—face at that moment.

'Oh, God,' she whispered shakily, 'I can't be in love with him, I just can't. . . .'

It couldn't have happened just like that. One minute hating him, the next—wanting him so badly that her whole body ached with the longing. And it wasn't only a physical thing. She wanted to be everything he had expected of her as his wife—mistress of his households, hostess to his friends and business associates, bearer of his children.

Why had she taken so long to recognise the signs that had been there for the noticing? The way his bronze moulded body pleasured her eyes, the way his slightest touch inflamed her senses and stirred the bitter-sweet delights of sensual desire, his consideration for servants who had been kind to him as a child, the respect and affection in which he was held by businessman and servant alike—not to mention his caring for her own father. There were a hundred reasons why she should love him. The only mystery was why she had wasted so much valuable time in realising her own vulnerability.

But it wasn't too late—surely it wasn't too late. She had found him kissing Francisca that night, but she was certain that intimacy had been the first since the other woman's return from France. And not all the Franciscas in the world could take him away from a wife he had possessed, the wife he was about to discover loved him in the way he had once told her he loved her. She could still win him back. . . .

Noise erupted into the courtyard beneath the windows of the bedroom, and there were the sounds of farewell and car doors closing, engines purring off into the night. Leaping from the bed with sudden joyous energy, Laurel rushed to the long bank of heavy wardrobes and wrenched one of the doors open, fingers fumbling in her haste as she unzipped the shimmering green dress she had worn for the dinner.

After wasting a few precious moments looking along the rack of nightdresses, her final selection was one of

gossamer purity in its whiteness ... the purity of her
innocence in sexual experience. Diego would discover
that anyway.

The pounding of her heart was suffocating when she
stood at last before the long mirror, knowing that she
had never looked more desirable as a woman. She had
loosened her hair and brushed it into gleaming silver
falls at either side of her flushed cheeks, and her eyes
held the deep shine of anticipation. Her fingers, long
and slender, ran lightly over the curves clearly outlined under the wispy full-length nightdress in the
knowledge that soon her hands would be replaced by
Diego's. A shiver ran over her skin and she turned from
the mirror, her step light as she went in bare feet to
straighten the rumpled covers on the bed, leaving them
invitingly open over the green silk sheets. Then, her
tongue dry with nervousness, she padded softly across
to switch off the main lights, leaving only two small wall
sconces above the dressing table and the bedside lamps
to cast their subdued light into the heavy atmosphere
of the room.

How she had hated it, this room, with its oppressively
black Spanish furniture, its air of brooding darkness
that had made her revert to childhood and leave the
wall sconces burning the night through.

Now she would share it with Diego, and his sleeping
body beside her in the enormous bed would be security
enough for her.

He was taking so long to come, she frowned, going to
draw aside the heavy brocade curtains covering the
softer lace next to the grilled window. Her heart leapt
at the thought that he was perhaps talking to the
Justice Minister after all, setting aside his ingrained
courtesy for her father's sake.

But the courtyard was empty of cars, apart from Diego's own Mercedes glinting silver under one of the elaborate wrought iron lamps surrounding the paved area. Breath stopped, then rushed in a sudden gust through her mouth when she saw Diego's unmistakable figure, the white sleeve of his jacket splashed across the black cape of the woman with him, walk slowly towards the car.

Laurel bit down so hard on her lower lip that she tasted blood when the pair halted beside the passenger door and Diego's other arm enfolded the woman so that she stood with raised face in the circle of his arms. Francisca!

When Diego's head began to bend towards the pale oval of the dark woman's face, Laurel cried out once in animal-like pain and dropped the curtains back in place with a hand that was nerveless.

The door must have been unlocked some time during the night, for when Laurel woke, her personal maid, the diminutive Teresa, had already left the usual early morning coffee tray on the bedside table, although the heavy curtains were still drawn across the high windows.

A touch on the silver pot telling her that the coffee was lukewarm, Laurel pushed her legs out of bed and stumbled to pull back the outer curtains, blinking when bright sunlight streamed into that half of the room. She stared dully at the hands of the ormolu clock on the mantel above the fireplace. The hands stood at a few minutes after nine. Was it possible she had slept so deeply and so long after spending what seemed like the entire night drowning herself in tears of misery?

The mirrored wall above the bathroom sinks made it clear that she hadn't dreamt the night away. The normally clear-cut outlines of her finely boned face were blurred and swollen, her eyes unbecomingly puffed from the access of tears. Some of the fiery redness and swelling disappeared when she bathed her face in iced water from the specially fitted tap, and her brain was clearer when she went back to the bedside table and poured coffee into the fluted cup. Tepid or not, its familiar taste was comforting.

As she wandered around cup in hand, shunning the bed that was as abhorrent to her now as it had been enticing the night before, her mind kept returning to the indisputable fact that Diego had not returned until dawn was streaking the sky—if he had returned at all! She would have heard the car, quiet though its engine ran.

But at least, by sleeping late, she had avoided the necessity to come face to face with him in stark daylight. There was no way he could have known of her elaborate preparations to receive him last night ... a wry laugh rasped bitterly in her throat. But there was humiliation enough in the knowledge that he had stayed with Francisca rather than come back to her room as he had promised.

She paced restlessly back to pour more coffee into the cup, and this time took it to one of the brocaded armchairs flanking the fireplace.

Of course he had to have come back some time during the night, or Teresa wouldn't have been able to come in with the coffee tray. Unless—the final humiliation of all!—he had left the key to his wife's locked door on the half table to one side of it in the passage outside.

Were the servants even now chattering and giggling among themselves at the *señor's bravura* in locking away his recalcitrant wife before going to his mistress?

But speculation must have been rife anyway about the fact that the *señor* did not share the matrimonial bedchamber with his *norte-americana* bride. Teresa was a simple, obliging girl, but she would have had to be *loca* not to notice that only Laurel slept in the bed which would have accommodated six comfortably.

The bed she had thought to share with Diego, the husband she had come to love, the man who had grown tired of his fruitless tie to her, who had rekindled the passion he had once felt for Francisca. And Francisca was now free to marry him. . . .

Fresh tears trembled on her lids when a peremptory knock came at the door. Before she had time to do more than rise precipitously to her feet, the door was thrust open and Diego, immaculately fresh in charcoal suit and crisp white shirt embellished with a red and grey striped tie, was standing only a few yards from her. She had forgotten the revealing nature of her nightgown until his vitally alive eyes swept her from head to toe in a purely masculine gaze that penetrated the misty folds of the gown and took in the total femininity of her curved form beneath it.

Laurel heard his swift intake of breath, and checked her own instinctive movement to cover herself. To a man coming from Francisca's voluptuous curves, her own must pale to insignificance. But she could do nothing to control the wild leaping of her pulses the sight of him provoked—tall, strong, and still exuding that air of sexual desirability despite his night of love with Francisca.

'Are you so unhappy, *querida*?' he asked roughly, making her aware of the fresh tears that had spilled from lid to cheek, standing there like frozen reminders of the life they might have shared.

Brushing them away with a brusque movement of her hand, she answered caustically: 'Unhappy, *señor*? Why should I be unhappy? I'm married to a man who is rich and powerful, and I'm the daughter of a man wrongfully accused of drug smuggling. What is there in my life to make me unhappy? One and one still make two, don't they? One powerful husband, one released father—isn't that the way it's supposed to go?'

'Laurel, I promise you——'

'Save your promises for Francisca,' she bit off harshly, animated enough now to walk confidently to the wardrobe and extract the negligee matching her nightdress.

'Francisca?'

His frown of uncomprehension could almost have been genuine, and she would have believed his bewilderment if she hadn't seen him leave with the attractive Mexican the night before.

'Francisca,' she returned flatly, fingers busily hooking small buttons into even smaller holes.

Diego took a step towards her. 'I can explain about Francisca.'

'No explanations necessary,' she cut him off crisply, finishing with the buttons at last and sitting before the mirrored dressing table to pull a brush through hair still tangled from the night before. 'All I want to know is how soon my father—and I—can leave this hellish country of yours.'

In the mirror she saw the familiar closing down of his expression, the subtle tightening of jaw and cheek

muscles that precluded even guesswork as to the state
of his emotions.

'I came to tell you,' he enunciated stiffly, 'that I have
made an appointment with José Perez, the Justice
Minister, for eleven o'clock this morning.'

'Oh.' For a moment the brush in Laurel's hand was
halted in mid-sweep. 'Well, you can let me know the
results of the meeting in Acapulco. I'm leaving on the
noon plane.'

Silence mounted between them until Diego broke the
tension that threatened to make her scream out all the
accusations she had formed during the long night when
she had sobbed into her pillow. The pillow Diego had
provided along with the food she ate, the expensive
clothes she wore, the skilled attention of the servants
he employed.

'You will go to Jacintha Point?' he queried now with
a proud lift of his black brows.

'I have no choice, have I?' Laurel responded bitterly,
throwing the brush away from her and turning to face
him. 'When you married me, I gave up my job and the
salary from it. Until I can contact Brent, I have no
choice but to rely on your generosity.'

The anger that had been subdued in his demeanour
since last night flared again in the black depths of his
eyes, but Laurel had no fear of his Latin temper now.
Almost she wished that he would snuff out the life that
had no meaning for her now without his love. And it
was only too evident from the pinched whiteness of
his mouth, the steely line of his jaw, that love was far
from his thoughts at that moment.

'So! I will keep you informed of developments here.
Meanwhile,' he crossed to the ivory telephone in its
nook close to the bedhead, 'I will reserve space for you

134 JACINTHA POINT

on the noon flight. I take it you have not already made a reservation?'

Laurel shook her head, watching the supple finger that dialled the requisite number, hearing the swift spate of Spanish which resulted in Diego's brief: 'Space has been reserved for you on the plane.'

Then he was dialling again, long distance this time, drumming his fingers restlessly on the wall beside the telephone until Juanita came on the line. His instructions to her were just as brief, and in two minutes he had replaced the receiver.

'Guillermo will meet you at the airport in Acapulco. Juanita will be prepared for your arrival.'

'Not Guillermo!' she said with involuntary sharpness. 'I—I'll take a cab from the airport, it isn't far.'

'I prefer that Guillermo collect you. There is little to occupy his energies on the boat while I am not there.'

Laurel shrugged mentally and let it rest there. Was it possible that Diego didn't know how Guillermo occupied his energies when the boss was away? She had met the good-looking young man just after the wedding, and recognised him immediately as one of the beach boys she had seen in Acapulco, the ones who successfully plied their trade with ageing women tourists. Diego would never let him near his wife if he knew about Guillermo's extra-curricular activities— but then perhaps he didn't care any more.

He had turned away when she halted his progress to the door. 'You'll keep me informed of developments in my father's case?'

'Naturalmente.'

Laurel doubted if he heard her whispered: 'Thank you,' as he went from the room. And why would he care? she questioned savagely. The sooner he was rid of her father and herself the sooner he would be united legally with Francisca, the woman who had married another man yet still had the power to sway a lover from way back. The woman who had come back to take up the shattered threads of her life, the dominant skein being Diego Ramirez.

CHAPTER NINE

Guillermo met her as scheduled, and while they drove the short distance to Jacintha Point Laurel was aware again, as she had been many times during the two week honeymoon period, of the young Mexican's admiration. He had made no overt approach to her while Diego was present at the resort home, but now his dark-eyed glance was boldly masculine when he said:

'Señor Diego is very trusting to let his beautiful wife travel so far alone.'

To Guillermo, Mexico City was light years away from the environment he had known all his life, and Laurel gave him a dry smile.

'It would have been difficult for anyone to kidnap me,' she told him lightly. 'I was driven to the airport in Mexico City by Señor Diego's chauffeur, spent an hour surrounded by other people on the plane, and you met me here. What possible harm could have come to me?' She forbore mentioning that Diego had lost that possessive air of Spanish men with their wives, which had made him frown on her going anywhere unaccompanied. Of course, this morning he had had the meeting with the Justice Minister, so was unable to accompany her to the airport himself.

For the rest of the journey she was preoccupied with thoughts of her father and how soon his trial might be arranged and his release processed. Not for one minute had she doubted his innocence. He had always been adamant in his opposition to the drug scene on any

level, and there was no way he would have been per-
suaded to assist men bent on quick and highly lucra-
tive profits in the drug trade.

If only the two who had chartered the boat had been
found! she pondered, biting on her lip. One way or the
other the truth could have been forced out of them.
Without them, Dan Trent was left literally holding the
bag.

Lost in the oppression of her thoughts, she hardly
noticed the tropical foliage and scrub they passed, and
in what seemed no time they were sweeping along the
crushed white rock drive to Jacintha Point. Juanita
appeared at the black-studded door, her welcome
courteous despite a faint air of puzzlement about her
dark features.

'Señor Diego is to come later?' she probed as she
followed Laurel into the master suite carrying her cosmetic case while Guillermo brought up the rear with
the one suitcase Laurel had considered necessary. The
majority of her clothes, the elegant day and evening
dresses bought by Diego to meet the requirements of
Mexican society, she had left behind in the Mexico
City house. She would never go back there.

'I—yes, he'll be coming later,' she lied to the housekeeper, who loved Diego like a son. There was no point
in disillusioning her about the marriage she had long
awaited before it was necessary to do so. It could still
be weeks before Dan, and she, would be free to leave
Mexico. 'He had some business details to see to in the
city.'

Juanita sighed. 'Ah, business! Always it comes first
with Señor Diego. Even as a boy he had a great sense
of duty, and cared for his brother Jaime like a father,
although there were few years between them. But

Jaime,' her eyes lifted heavenward, 'had no wish to be
told by his brother. He wanted to laugh and take enjoyment from life, with no thought for tomorrow.'

'Did their parents never come with them?' Laurel
gave in to the curiosity she seldom indulged.

The housekeeper shrugged plump shoulders, a shutter coming down over her features as she turned to the
door. 'They died when Señor Diego was a boy. After
that, Señora Jacintha came to be with her grandsons
sometimes.' She looked back from the door. 'What time
will you take dinner, *señora*?'

Laurel clicked open her vanity case on the dressing
table. 'Oh, around eight-thirty will be fine, Juanita, but
I'd like to have *merienda* in the small *sala* at four.' The
afternoon refreshment custom was a welcome one in the
long break between lunch and dinner. 'I'll be going
out after that for a while.'

'Out, *señora*?' Juanita frowned. 'You will require
Guillermo to drive you somewhere?'

'No, I'll drive myself,' Laurel returned firmly, doing
her best to ignore the housekeeper's irritating assumption that a woman, even if married, laid herself open
to the amorous advances of men if she ventured out
alone. In any case, she was sure that the servants at
Jacintha Point were unaware of her father's incarceration in the local jail, and she wasn't about to enlighten
them on that point. 'Was there any mail for me?' she
changed the subject with forced casualness.

'No, *señora*.'

'All right. *Gracias*, Juanita.'

So Brent hadn't replied to her letter enclosing his
ring—but then she hadn't really expected him to or, if
she was honest, wanted him to. Even back then she
must have known that all her horizons were filled with

Diego, that the affection she had felt for Brent was just that. There had never been any wild clamour of her senses when Brent's hand brushed hers unintentionally, no agonised pain of parting as she was suffering now because Diego would soon no longer be part of her life.

The irony of it hit her like a hammerblow as she lay stretched out on top of the bedcovers, clad only in the white slip she had worn under her travelling suit, one arm curved around her head as she stared fixedly at the elaborately scrolled ceiling. When Diego had wanted to make love to her in this bed she had fought him— or had she in reality been fighting her own desire to surrender to the quick passion his lovemaking had roused in her? Wantonness had never been a part of her nature until that night, when Diego had swamped her senses and carried her along on a tide of desire that was almost unbearable. . . .

'*Perdon, señora! Señora,* the telephone!'

Laurel woke drowsily to the sound of Juanita's anxious voice and light touch on her shoulder. 'Mmm? What is it, Juanita?'

'The telephone, *señora.* They say the *policia.*' The woman's awed tones penetrated Laurel's consciousness at last, and she sat up suddenly on the bed, swinging her legs to the floor and pushing back her hair with one suddenly trembling hand.

'Police?' she echoed, wild thoughts churning through her mind. Was it possible that Diego's talk with the Justice Minister had borne fruit so quickly?

'I'll take it here, Juanita.'

Despite the excitement that made her hand tremble almost uncontrollably, she waited until she heard the click of the hall receiver being replaced before announcing herself.

'*Perdon, señora,*' the disembodied male voice apologised, 'it is Señor Ramirez I wish to speak with.'

'He isn't here, he's in Mexico City. But I——'

'Then if you would give me a telephone number where I can reach him, *señora*, I will be grateful.'

'If it's something to do with my father, Daniel Trent, I can take the message,' Laurel snapped in irritation, railing inwardly once more at the Latin presumption that women were helpless in matters of business, and gritting her teeth when the official repeated his request for Diego's telephone number. Tersely, she rattled off the numbers for home and office, then added:

'I'm coming down right now to see my father. Maybe he'll tell me what's going on.'

'That would not be advisable, *señora*,' the smooth voice said into her ear.

'What do you mean, not advisable? You can't stop me from seeing my own father!'

'It would be a wasted journey, Señora Ramirez. Your father is—not here.'

Laurel stared blankly at the telephone. 'Not there? I don't understand. He can't have been moved already.'

'*Si.* He has gone.'

Sudden wild joy leapt along her veins and left her breathless. Who said the Mexican wheels of justice grind slowly? Diego had spoken to the Minister just hours ago, and already her father was on his way to a speedy trial—probably in Mexico City.

'Thank you, *gracias, señor*,' she bubbled into the mouthpiece, and scarely heard his murmured reply. Dropping the receiver back in its cradle, she danced a pirouette across the floor.

Suddenly she stopped, her bare arms coming round to hug her waist. Dan's trial and probable release also brought the termination of her marriage to Diego. But she couldn't—mustn't—think about that right now. She had discovered her love too late, and Francisca was the one he wanted now.

From the window she looked down across the flagged terrace to the north bay where the water surged and fell back in a froth of creamy spray. She had never swum on either of the beaches, and she would like to do that before leaving Jacintha Point. Her plans would have to be changed now, of course, although she might have to wait here another day before knowing definitely where Dan had been taken.

Spurred into action, she took the briefest bikini she possessed from the drawer. No one in the world would see her if she lay well back from the shore under the overhang of the coconut palms, and it made no difference what she wore in the water.

Juanita appeared in answer to her ring, and she told the housekeeper that instead of *merienda* in the house, she would take a flask of orange juice to the beach.

'The Señora will not be going out in the car?' the housekeeper eyed the length of slender legs beneath the short terrycloth beach jacket.

'No, I find I don't have to go after all.' Laurel picked up her sunglasses from the dresser and slid them on to her nose, then searched in her bag for the paperback book she had tried vainly to read on the plane.

'There is no trouble?' Juanita asked with wary dignity, and Laurel swung round, surprised. 'The *policia*—the telephone call.'

'Oh. No, no trouble. They—they wanted to speak with Señor Diego, so I gave the telephone numbers in Mexico City.'

'So!' Satisfied, Juanita went off to the kitchen for

the orange juice while Laurel finished packing the
capacious straw beach bag with blanket, towel, book
and suntan lotion. The last she held loosely in her hand
for several moments, remembering that it was from this
same bottle that Diego had taken the cream to rub into
her skin. She shivered, remembering the oiled smoothness of his hands at her nape, her shoulders, breasts ...
hastily, she pushed the bottle to the bottom of the bag
and hoisted it over her shoulder.

The water was only a degree or two cooler than the air
temperature, but Laurel welcomed its languorous
warmth, the buoyancy that made swimming effortless,
and she alternately swam, then floated on her back
across the lagoon-like bay. The sleek white of Diego's
yacht hove into view, and she wondered idly if Guillermo had returned to the boat after meeting her at the
airport.

After half an hour she had had enough and idled her
way back to shore where the cooled orange juice
awaited her. A pat or two with the thick towel was
ample; the sun would soon dry the dampened darkness
of the bikini strips back to their original shade of light
tan, a colour that matched the pale gold of her skin so
perfectly she might have been wearing nothing at all.

She lay back on the vividly patterned blanket, prop-
ping herself on one elbow while she sipped slowly from
the flask cup. Time stretched like a tunnel before her.
How many times in the years to come would she summon the memory of this scene?—the startling white of
sand so fine it was like silk underfoot; the light
greenish-blue of water that caressed her woman's flesh
like the encompassing embrace of a lover's arms; the
jagged rocks that swept to the Point and petered out

reluctantly where they met the sea; even the coconut palms above her head where the fruit hung ripe under the dark green fronds.

Replacing the cup, she lay back completely and closed her eyes against the fierce rays of the sun. She should rub lotion into her skin, she acknowledged drowsily, and she would in just a minute. . . .

A shadow fell across her face and her eyes snapped open in heart-pounding panic. For a wild moment she thought it was Diego who stood there in white cotton shirt open to the waist and skin-tight faded jeans frayed at the cuffs. The head, silhouetted against a background of blazing sun, almost had the shape of Diego's, but the hair was longer.

'Guillermo?' she gasped, jackknifing herself into a sitting position and groping for the beach jacket which contrarily eluded her grasp. 'What are you doing here?'

'Juanita was concerned that you might need something,' he said softly as if he spoke through a mist, and Laurel felt his gaze slope down over her body with its brief strips of cloth, realising with sudden cold clarity that they only served to emphasise all that was female about her.

'I don't believe you. Juanita knows I have everything I need.'

Undeterred, Guillermo bent to a crouching position and looked knowingly into her eyes. 'Does she, señora? Do you think she does not see what I myself have seen? The señor has taken a beautiful wife, one any man would be proud to have in his bed, yet he sends her from him with a sadness in her eyes. I know the look well, señora. I have seen it in the eyes of the women who came to Acapulco without their husbands.'

Life suddenly sparkled back into Laurel's limbs and

she leapt furiously to her feet. 'I'm sure you do,' she said with a contemptuous gesture of her hand. 'But I'm not one of the tourists you pick up on the beaches of Acapulco. When I tell my husband——'

'There is no need to tell the *señor*,' he said in a knowingly persuasive way, his voice lowering to huskiness. 'I can make you happy, *señora*, I know how.'

'And I know how to get Carlos down here,' Laurel blazed, opening her mouth to scream Carlos's name, but the yell turned to a squeak when Guillermo reached for her arm and jerked her violently against him, covering her mouth with his free hand.

Silently they struggled, fright lending power to the clenched fist and elbow of Laurel's right arm until Guillermo grunted and took his hand from her mouth. For the flash of a few seconds they glared into each other's eyes, hesitation showing briefly in his. Laurel took advantage of it to open her mouth for another scream, but Guillermo leaned forward almost desperately to cover it with a hard thrust of his lips that sent them both swaying precariously on the hot sand.

No match for his superior strength, Laurel fought now against the rising nausea his nearness caused. The pungent odour of sweat from his hard young body filled her nostrils and made her senses reel off into faintness. If only Carlos, or even Juanita, would come to the top of the steps cut out of the rocks! Her neck felt as if it would snap from the pressure of the grinding kiss that seemed to be going on for ever. . . .

Then suddenly she was free—so suddenly that she fell to her knees in the sand, seeing dimly through a red haze that Guillermo was picking himself up from the beach an incredible distance away, heard the string of oaths uttered in only too comprehensible Spanish,

looked up and saw the icy fury that had leached the
colour from her saviour's skin.

'Diego!' she sobbed. 'Oh, Diego!'

Through the blur of tears she saw his face turn down
to hers, but her swimming eyes obscured his expression.
All her shocked mind noted was that he was in-
congruously dressed for the beach in his business suit,
white shirt and red and grey tie. Was it possible that
she had conjured up the vision of him because she had
needed him so?

She brushed a hand across her eyes and saw that it
was indeed a flesh and blood Diego who stood there,
and that he had turned away again to glare venomously
at Guillermo, who looked down on them from half way
up the steps, holding out placating hands.

'It was not my fault, *señor*,' he whined shakily. 'Your
wife asked me to——'

'Go!' Diego thundered. 'Get back to the boat, I will
speak with you later.'

His eyes remained fixed on the cliff until Guillermo
had leapt up the remaining steps and disappeared.
Only then did he turn back to the frozen Laurel, still
kneeling on the sand at his feet, her breath catching at
sight of the frightening depth of fury reflected in his
eyes.

'Get up!' he told her harshly, making no effort to
help raise her, and she stared disbelievingly up at the
face carved from granite.

'You don't believe him?' she questioned in a whisper.

'Get up,' he repeated, his eyes flicking contemptuously over the briefness of the bikini as she stumbled
to her feet. The bikini that looked as if it was part of
her. 'It makes no difference whether or not I believe
Guillermo. What do you expect of a young man who

sees an attractive woman lying almost naked on a
deserted beach?'

'Not what I got!' Laurel's reflexes flared to life again.
She lifted an arm to push back her tangled hair.

'No?' Diego's eyes narrowed on the raised swell of
her breast scantily covered by the bikini and she
dropped her arm quickly to her side. She was unsure of
him in this mood. Anger at times burned deep inside
his volatile nature, but now there was something im-
placable about him, about the way he tugged his tie
loose and discarded it along with his jacket on the sand.
His hands went next to the buttons on his shirt.

'Wh-what are you doing?'

'I am preparing to take pleasure with my wife, who
gives freely to other men what she denies me.' His shirt
followed the other items of clothing, and he bent to
pull off his shoes and socks, bronze shoulders rippling
with the effort. When he straightened and reached for
the belt around his waist, Laurel turned and fled across
the sand.

It was no real contest. Diego cut across immediately
to the firmer packed shoreline and followed its curve
until he was level with Laurel, then cut in towards her.
His forward tackle toppled both of them to the
powdery sand, his weight pressing the length of her
back and legs abrasively against the fine, gritty par-
ticles. Pain seared her skin from the trapped heat of a
sun that had beaten down on the beach all day long,
and she turned agonised eyes up to Diego's menacing
face.

'Please—you're hurting me,' she pleaded breathlessly. 'Let me up.'

His eyes flickered to the dazzling surface surrounding them, then he glanced up and back to where her

blanket was spread under the palms.

'*Si*,' he agreed huskily. 'If we are to come together like peasants, it is better that we have at least the comfort of a blanket.'

Laurel's immediate plan to walk casually beside him, making a break close to the steps so that she could run up them and call, scream, for one of the servants was foiled when Diego lifted her easily into his arms and strode off across the sand with her.

The feel of his hot, hard flesh against hers seared her in a different way than had the sun-baked beach, and panic rippled through her. She had wanted him, had her sleep haunted by dreams of his possession—but not like this, not when he was inspired by a lust to even the score with the men whose intimacies he imagined she had invited. And she had not forgotten Francisca, although it was evident from the set, determined expression on Diego's smooth-planed face that the other woman was far from his thoughts.

Her hand sought the support of his tensed shoulder muscle, feeling its hard smooth texture against her palm. The faint scent of aftershave lotion lingered on his facial skin, overriding the purely male odour of recently acquired sweat.

'Please ... Diego,' she whispered. 'Not like this.'

As if she had said nothing, he dropped her to the blanket and completed his own disrobement, his closed expression revealing nothing of shame or regret at his frankly aroused nudity, only an impatiently significant sweep of his eyes over the tantalising brevity of her bikini. He dropped to his knees, and even that covering modesty was stripped from her in two brief movements that left her vulnerably exposed to the raking inspec-

tion of eyes that flared and burned with a primitive
emotion.

'Diego, don't. . . .'

Lowering his body until it half lay over hers, and
sliding a hand under her head so that her face tilted
towards his, he taunted:

'Soon you will be saying "Diego, do" in the manner
of all wives who desire their husbands.' His voice grew
thick. 'When I kiss you here,' his mouth reached for
and found the soft flesh cradling her pelvis and traced
a hot line to the gentle hollow of her navel, where his
tongue lingered briefly before his head moved upward
again over her midriff, 'and here,' his mouth fastened
on the rounded swell of her breast, shooting urgent
sensations through her sensitised nerve ends and making her hands clutch convulsively at the blue-black
head bent to elicit just that response from her. A strand
of his hair fell forward over his brow as he raised his
head and continued huskily:

'And here.'

Laurel's mouth lifted of its own accord to meet the
unhurried descent of his, opening in ardent submission
to his male seeking. Logical thought skittered away
under the hard persuasion of lips schooled by in-
heritance to rouse a woman to passionate desire. Then
there was nothing except the warm tangle of their
bodies, a mutual exploration fanned by the mounting
flame of desire that consumed them and sent Laurel's
hands with swift sensuous strokes along the ridged
muscles of his back, feeling its moistness under her
palms and glorying in the new-found sense of power
that made her aware of her woman's ability to match
the passion leaping from his veins to hers.

And all the time she was conscious of the gentle yet

relentless swish of the ocean as it rose and fell on the hardpacked shore ... pain was a short, exquisite agony that led to an explosion of uninhibited delight spreading upwards through her....

'*Cristo!*' Diego's expression as he leaned over her was strained, his eyes reflecting a mixture of triumphantly sated passion and disbelief. 'You were—a *virgen*,' he resorted to his own language as if not trusting English to express the depth of his meaning. 'Yet you told me——'

Laurel rushed in breathlessly when he paused, her eyes a bright glow of iridescent green as they darted from his proudly curved mouth to the heavy lidded darkness of his eyes. 'Oh, Diego, I told you that because I—I didn't know then that I—that——'

As she struggled for words to tell him how she had fought against acknowledging, even to herself, the attraction he had held for her from the beginning, before he had literally blackmailed her into marriage, she heard the sough of wind in the palm tree above them, saw the quick lift of his head, heard the muffled exclamation as his arm lifted in a defensive movement, and felt a moment of panic before utter darkness blotted out consciousness....

CHAPTER TEN

FLAME-COLOURED gladioli, their blossoms like huge orchids studding the stiff stems, filled her line of vision for a long time before she became aware of the white blur hovering outside the perimeter of her immediate vicinity.

'Hello?' she called tentatively, the sound reverberating in her head although the white figure seemed impervious to its loudness. It must be the thirst, she thought dazedly, feeling the dryness coat her mouth and the surface of her throat. Visions of iced drinks floated before her, sharpening her thirst until she groaned with frustrated longing.

This time the plea was heard, and a woman's concerned face, encircled by a halo of white, materialised from the shadowed depths.

'Thanks be to God,' a gentle voice murmured in a language Laurel knew instinctively was not her own, yet its translation came easily to her. 'You have need of something, my child?'

Laurel signalled her craving for a cooling drink, and the white figure dissolved into the background to reappear within minutes with a liquid so cold that she choked on it.

'Your husband will be happy to know that you are again with us,' the gentle voice went on in the same language.

'*Mi esposo?*' Laurel queried, a frown settling between her brows. 'I have a husband?'

'But of course. He has been much worried about you.' The white lady seemed to be having difficulty with the language she had switched to, as if she had just remembered that Spanish was not the mother tongue of the girl who appeared so fragile and slender under the light covering of sheet and blanket. 'I will tell him of your recovery and bring him to you.'

Laurel halted her swift withdrawal. 'Please—wait. Who is he? I—I don't seem to remember. . . .'

'You are the wife of Señor Ramirez,' the answer came edged with respect. 'The Señor is an important man in Mexico.'

Mexico. What was she doing here, evidently married to a man of Mexican origin? Unaware of murmuring the question, she was immediately reprimanded.

'You are the wife of Señor Diego Ramirez,' the soft voice chided. 'There was an accident on the beach below this house, Jacintha Point.'

Accident? Jacintha Point? The words meant nothing to Laurel, and she shook her head in bewilderment, feeling its dull ache as a heaviness behind her forehead. Her brows drew down in a painful frown. 'I can't seem to—remember.'

'Do not concern yourself, *señora*. It is to be expected that there will be some difficulty after such an accident. Rest quietly now, and I will tell the *señor* that you are conscious once more.'

Laurel's hand groped for and found the starched white sleeve. 'Please,' she whispered, 'tell me about the accident first.' The thought of facing an unknown husband was terrifying in the extreme. Who was he, what was he like? Was he young, or old as his apparent standing indicated? For that matter, who was she?

'You were lying on the beach, *señora*, foolishly under

the ripened fruits of a coconut palm. Many times skulls
have been crushed by a falling fruit.'

'That's—what happened to me?'

'It was fortunate that the Señor was with you at the
time,' a faint pink covered the pale cheeks. 'He was able
to avert most of the force from the missile. And now,
señora, I will bring him to you. It was only this morning that we were able to persuade him to rest, and that
only on condition that he was to be awakened at the
slightest change in your condition. *Perdon, señora*.'

Before Laurel could protest more the nurse faded
into the background and she was left with a tumult of
unanswered questions. How long had she been married to this Mexican man who had gone without rest
for—how long? He must love her very much.... She
should have asked the nurse for a mirror before she
brought her husband to her. Her soft underlip was
caught softly between her teeth. She didn't even know
what she looked like! Was her hair fair or dark, her
eyes blue or brown? She lifted a hand to touch the
textured silk beside her face, but there was no way of
telling from that whether it was ebony black or mouse
brown. Her fingers explored the contours of her face,
and she was wincing as they reached the tender spot
above her eyes when she suddenly became aware of a
man who had come silently to stand beside the bed.

At least she could see that he was dark-haired and
eyed, that the skin over his finely planed face was olive
in colour, and that he was in his early thirties. A brown
short-sleeved shirt was stretched to capacity over a
smoothly muscled chest, and beige slacks clung to lean
hips and taut thighs. The black eyes were sober as they
rested on her, and lines of fatigue radiated from them
and slashed in white streaks from high-bridged nose to

firmly held mouth. His eyes darkened still more when they shifted to the area surrounding hers.

'Laurel,' he said huskily, putting forward a long well-shaped hand to cover hers. So her name was Laurel! She was glad; it had a nice ring to it. What had the nurse said his name was?

'Diego,' she murmured, and saw a sudden gleam come into his eyes.

'You know me, *querida*?'

The light faded when she shook her head slightly. 'The—nurse told me.' Her gaze filtered down to a tightly wound bandage round his wrist, its whiteness stark against the tan of his sinewy arm. 'You've been hurt,' she wondered.

'It is nothing.'

'Did it happen when I got this?' she pointed to her head. 'The nurse said you—averted a worse accident to me.'

His mouth tightened grimly. 'It was my fault such an accident took place at all. I should have known. . . .'

Laurel stared blankly into the expressive darkness of his eyes as he broke off and sat abruptly beside her on the bed, his weight drawing down the mattress under her. There was something of significance underlying his words, but her brain refused to co-operate.

'How—how long have I been unconscious?' she asked, her voice sounding small and far away.

'For three days.' The raven blackness of his head moved sideways, his eyes dropping to the carpeted floor, the lines around his mouth deepening. Laurel turned her palm upward and clasped the hand that still lay over hers.

'You must be so tired,' she said gently. 'The nurse told me you had sat with me all that time.'

For several moments he stared broodingly at the hands clasped together on the coverlet, then as if the touch of her skin repelled him, he rose abruptly, leaving her fingers still curved upward.

'The doctor will be here soon.' His tone had a deadly impersonal quality, and Laurel frowned painfully, wishing her head would stop its aching. She couldn't think clearly with a thousand tiny hammers beating a tattoo on her brain. 'I will return when he has seen you.'

It seemed for a brief moment that he might bend and kiss her; instead, he turned and strode quickly away, leaving her puzzled and with an inexplicable prickle of tears behind her eyes.

If he was her husband, the man who had kept a solitary vigil at her bed for three days, why hadn't he wanted to stay with her now?

Laurel scattered crumbs from her breakfast rolls on the parapet edging the flowered terrace, smiling when the small, prettily coloured birds swooped from the nearby shrubbery and quarrelled noisily over the minute morsels.

'You are spoiling them, *niña*,' Diego said from the table behind her, a smile in his voice.

'They're so beautiful,' she murmured, turning back to him after brushing the last of the crumbs from her palms. 'I guess,' she reflected, taking her seat opposite him and reaching for the coffee pot, 'it's like having children. It must be so easy to give them everything they ask for. Would you like some?'

'Children?' he asked, his eyes startled and somewhat wary as they met hers across the table.

'No, silly, I'm offering you coffee.'

'Oh. Please.'

'Though come to think of it,' she went on slowly as she poured from the glinting silver pot, 'children wouldn't be such a bad idea either.'

She saw the familiar frown slice down between his brows.

'I thought we had agreed that such discussions could wait until you have recovered.' Diego took a slim cigar from the case and dropped his eyes to its tip as he lit it.

'You proposed that and I went along with it.' Laurel got up and moved restlessly back to the parapet, leaning with both hands on its sunwarmed surface and looking pensively out to the view of azure sky and turquoise ocean—a view that was totally familiar to her because it was the only one she knew. 'Diego?' she asked without turning.

'Yes?'

'Suppose my memory never does come back?'

The words hung between them brittly in the shimmering, heat-hazed air.

'The doctors have said it is only a matter of time.'

'Time!' she scorned, turning her back on the view to face Diego's lean-featured face. 'It's been almost two months, and all I get is the odd flash of a boat surrounded by a thousand just like it tied up at a pier, or a picture of nuns praying in a chapel somewhere.'

'You were educated in a convent,' Diego said carefully, edging the ash from his cigar into the tray at his hand.

Weary of the long weeks of probing her mind and coming up with only a headache, Laurel snapped: 'Why can't you tell me the things I need to know? Maybe something would ring a bell somewhere.'

Diego tossed the cigar into the ashtray and rose

abruptly, coming across to her, suavely good-looking
in pearl grey silk shirt and the mid-blue trousers of the
tropical suit he would wear in Mexico City that day.
His fingers burned like fire as they came to rest on her
upper arms, bare in a sleeveless top of yellow and white
stripes.

'You know that the doctors have told me not to explain the past to you,' he said patiently. 'It is best if you
remember naturally, without shock to the system.'

'Did they also tell you not to sleep with me?' Laurel
demanded, head tipped back challengingly to look into
his eyes, hating herself when they dropped darkly to
the outline of her mouth before flickering upward
again. The line of his jaw tightened to a steel band.

'No. That was my decision.' His hands dropped away
from her and he turned to the table to gather up the
papers he had been working on there. 'I must leave
now, Laurel, I have appointments this afternoon.'

She let his long-legged figure stride away but caught
up with him at the entrance to the master suite, following him into the smaller bedroom where he slept
in the single bed between two narrow windows overlooking the side view of cliffs and curving white beach.

'Can't I come with you this time?'

Diego looked round distractedly from where he was
packing papers into a black leather briefcase. 'It is
better if you stay here where it is quiet and peaceful.'
His courteous dismissal, one of many in the weeks since
her accident, flicked a dangerously raw nerve and
Laurel's head reared back angrily.

'And where I won't run into your mistress, is that it?'

The fastenings on the briefcase snapped shut and
Diego crossed the room to her, his expression unread-

able as his eyes roved quickly over the excited pink of
her cheeks.

'It is business, not romance, that takes me to Mexico
City,' he told her with a dryness born of long-suffering
patience.

Had he told her that before? Laurel suppressed the
instinct to cover her ears with her palms, as she had so
many times lately. Was it possible for a blow from a
falling coconut to disorientate her senses to the point
of madness? Or was it their unnatural mode of existence, with Diego behaving more like a concerned
brother than a husband and lover? That their relationship had been a normal one before the accident was
patent to her. Whenever he came near, her body quickened to the rhythm of remembered passion between
them, to a man who had plumbed every depth and
scaled every height with her.

'Diego?'

Her whispered mention of his name brought Diego
to a halt in the process of giving her the light kiss on
the forehead she had come to expect on his departure,
and he looked quizzically down into her face.

'Don't you think I might get better quicker if—if
we——' Her breath came in an impatient sigh. 'Surely
we had a normal relationship before the accident? In
fact, I know we did.'

His eyes narrowed on her upturned face. 'How do
you know that?' he asked tersely.

'How? Because I feel it,' she shrugged. 'You're my
husband, and I—I want you to make love to me. Is that
so wrong?'

He was silent for a moment, then he sighed heavily.
'No, *querida*, it is not wrong.' His voice softened to a
kind of tenderness. His hand left her shoulder to stroke

lightly against her silver hairline. 'Do you not think
that I, too, want to make love to you? It hasn't been
easy, Laurel, to be so close to you without coming to
your bed.'

'Then why?' she cried, twisting out of his grasp but
staying within his orbit. 'You're being too careful.
Physically I'm fine, so why——?'

'We will see when I return.'

Like a child being offered a delayed treat, Laurel
fumed silently, but she knew Diego well enough now
to know that he would not be swayed once he had made
up his mind.

But at least he had kissed her on the lips when he
left, she reflected later in her own room. Usually he
gave her a fatherly peck on the forehead, and the same
on his return. And a father was far from what she
needed right now. She wanted a husband, a lover, to
make her forget the nagging doubts and worries that
beset her whenever she was alone. That she had no
family to worry about her Diego had told her, but
surely she must have had a past with friends, acquaintances, other family members? No one had enquired
about her as far as she knew—but then maybe she had
dropped all prior ties when she married Diego. And
he would tell her nothing, content to wait until her
memory returned of its own accord, whenever that
might be.

The woven tapestry of the colourful bedspread was
rough under her fingers when she sat on the huge bed
which seemed even more enormous at night when she
was alone. Swinging her feet up, she lay back against
the downy pillows and stared up at the scrolled ceiling.
She knew every twist and turn of the plaster intimately,
she thought wryly, from all the hours when she had

lain probing a memory that refused to budge apart
from a few disjointed flashes of illumination.

Did Diego have a mistress in Mexico City? From
somewhere she knew that many Mexican men thought
nothing of supporting in luxury women not their wives.
And Diego was a passionate man—that much was obvious from even a casual inspection of his dark, expressive eyes, the smoothly muscled body that evoked
visions of his sensual nature. Few women would be able
to resist him, any more than she herself could when he
was near her. All her senses then were alert to his
attractions, only to be stifled by his courteous rejection
of her advances. However courteous the rejection, it
still hurt down in the secret recesses of her woman's
body.

But she didn't have to accept the chaste life forced
on her by the convent which Diego had told her had
educated her. She was married, with all the urges of a
normal woman in love with her husband.

Her mind furiously awake, Laurel began to plan.

She left nothing to chance. In the three days following
Diego's departure she had prepared not only the house,
but herself for his return. The gleaming silver on the
table was reflected in the sheen she had coaxed into hair
too long exposed to the harsh rays of the sun, the white
linen cloth was echoed in the purity of the bodice-high
dress against the even tan of her skin, her nails were
shaped and coloured to match the low centrepiece of
soft pink roses.

Making a last-minute check of the table with Juanita,
she turned shining eyes to the housekeeper. 'As soon as
Señor Diego arrives we'll have drinks in here. Will that

give you enough time to put the finishing touches to dinner?'

Juanita beamed. '*Si, señora.* The Señor always tells me he must take me to Mexico City to show his French chef how to make *enchiladas* the right way.'

'Then I know you must cook them perfectly, because Jules is a fantastic chef.' The telephone rang in the hall, and Laurel abstractedly paid little attention when Juanita went to answer it.

Everything would be perfect for her seduction scene; soft lights, good wine and her husband's favourite Mexican meal. Smiling wryly, she corrected the drooping angle of one rose and reflected that most wives required no special preparations to make their husbands desire them. Except perhaps the ones who had to wrest him from the arms of a mistress....

'The telephone, *señora*,' Juanita said from the door, her face showing the sympathy she felt. 'Señor Diego.'

'Señor——?' Laurel stared blankly at her. 'Oh. He wants me to pick him up at the airport?'

'The call is from Mexico City, *señora*.'

Disappointment welled up in Laurel's throat so that her voice was unnaturally strained when she picked up the receiver.

'Diego, you're not coming until later?'

Even through the disappointment, his attractively husky tone had the power to stir her. 'I am sorry, *querida*, it is not possible for me to come at all tonight.'

'But why? Everything's all ready ...'

'I am sorry, Laurel,' he apologised again, sounding remote now, 'but something has come up here that needs my attention. I will be with you on Sunday afternoon at the latest.'

'Sunday?' she queried, aghast.

'I have meetings tonight and a day full of them to-morrow.' His voice became lightly amused. 'Your countrymen regard work as something that takes precedence over weekends or vacations. And for this particular business deal, I must go along with them, however much I—I might want to be with you.'

'I see.' Laurel bit her lip. 'Then I can expect you on Sunday?'

'Certainly. If there is any change, I will call you again.'

The remainder of the short conversation was lost to Laurel as her mind turned over the possibility that for some reason Diego didn't want to come home. That thought was only a step away from the speculation that there was a woman he was reluctant to leave in the City. One he might have told about the wife who was now agitating for marriage in all its fullness.

No, it couldn't be so, she told herself as she instructed the mournful Juanita to serve dinner for one. Latin men were notorious for their strong sense of family, their ultimate loyalty to the women they made their wives. It really was business that had kept Diego away from her.

But his phone call the next evening postponing his return until Tuesday sent the sparks of suspicion flaming anew in her brain.

'I am sorry, Laurel,' his soft voice insinuated in her ear, 'but more meetings are necessary on Monday. If I stay here until Tuesday evening to take care of normal business, I will be free to spend a full week at Jacintha Point.'

'Don't bother on my account,' Laurel snapped in her disappointment, adding childishly before slamming down the receiver: 'Enjoy the weekend with your mistress!'

If he called back to refute the allegation she would tell Juanita that she would speak to no one, not even the Señor. But there was no return call. Proving, she told herself as she paced the luxurious blue bedroom carpet, that she had struck home with her conjecture.

So what was she supposed to do? Sit home and wait for her Latin husband's return from his mistress? Desperately she longed to be free of that humiliation, but there was nothing she could do about it. She was virtually a prisoner of her lost memory. She wouldn't know where to go or who to contact if she left the understated luxury of Jacintha Point.

Her dreams, waking or sleeping, were punctuated by visions of the woman Diego was spending the weekend with in Mexico City. Always the woman was voluptuously dark, the antithesis of herself. But why, if Diego preferred that type of woman, would he have married her? She had the Nordic fairness of cooler climes, her figure slender while women of his own race possessed the abundant curves presumably desired by Mexican men.

Often she pressed her fingers to her temples, uselessly trying to remember. Perhaps their marriage had been on the point of breaking up before the accident. That could explain Diego's reluctance to resume the intimacies of the relationship they had once had.

And then on Monday, when the circumference of her world encompassed only the azure sky and blue-green sea, remembrance was brutally forced on her. . . .

'*Señora!* A visitor.'

Intent on capturing the cavorting outlines of the

gaily coloured birds fighting over the crumbs she had
scattered over the balustrade, Laurel at first ignored the
housekeeper's peremptory call for her attention. The
watercolour paints Diego had suggested as a diversion
for the times when he would necessarily be away had
been a brainwave on his part. She loved the challenge
of trying to capture the bright plumage of birds who
had evidently never heard of still life compositions.

'*Señora!*' Juanita implored again. 'There is a visitor.'

'Don't bother,' a male voice interrupted from behind
Juanita's sturdy figure. 'I'll speak to Miss Trent—
Señora Ramirez!—myself.'

Laurel screwed up her eyes against the sun outlining
the visitor's head and felt a familiar pang behind her
temples. It was the flashing pain that prepared the
sudden arrival of a scene from her past, gone before she
could grasp its import. Yet this man, obviously an
American, evidently knew her. He had called her—
what? Miss Trent. Excitement brought a thin film of
perspiration to her upper lip. Was it possible he could
throw a knowledgeable light on her past?

'It's all right, Juanita,' she told the hovering housekeeper. 'I'll talk with Señor——?' She looked per-
plexedly at the tall young man still haloed by the sun.

'Laurel! It's me—Brent! Don't tell me you've forgotten me so soon.'

When he stepped forward to face her at the balustrade, Laurel felt a pang of disappointment. She didn't
know the good-looking young man with his straight
fair hair and hazel eyes. Yet. . . .

'Bring some coffee,' she told the disapproving
Juanita, then wiped the paint from her stained fingers.
'I'm sorry, I don't recognise you.'

'You must be kidding! It's me, Laurel—Brent Halliday. We were engaged once, remember? Although I must say,' he cast a calculating look around the flower filled terrace and out to the Pacific view beyond, 'you knew what you were doing when you threw me over for Ramirez.'

'Th-threw you over?' she stammered, then caught sight of the still lingering housekeeper. 'Juanita, I asked you to bring coffee.'

'*Si, señora,*' the dark-skinned woman answered sulkily before moving off to the patio doors.

Laurel looked assessingly at the young American, then gestured with unconscious grace to the patio table near them. 'Please sit down. Juanita shouldn't be long with coffee. She's been a little protective of me since the accident,' she apologised, pulling out one of the wrought iron chairs and sinking on to its padded seat.

'Accident? What accident?'

Laurel laughed lightly, indicating the seat opposite. 'Yes. A stupid one. I was lying under a coconut palm on the beach down there,' she gestured backwards with her hand, 'and one of the coconuts fell and hit me.' She took off her sunglasses in deference to the umbrella shading the table area. 'Since then I haven't been able to remember a thing. Please do sit down.'

The man sank on to the chair as if his legs would no longer support him, and his face was whitely strained as he looked across the table into the sea-green eyes.

'You mean—you can't remember *anything*?'

'Not a thing. Well,' she corrected hastily, 'I do get the odd flash of remembrance, but nothing that means very much to me. A boat tied up at a pier, nuns singing in a chapel, that kind of thing. The doctors say it will all come back in time. But——' she hesitated. Would it be right to ask this man, who obviously knew her from the

past, about things which Diego and the doctors believed were better uncovered naturally?

'You really don't know me, do you?' he said wonderingly, looking round abstractedly when Juanita re-
appeared in double quick time with the coffee tray.
When the Mexican woman had reluctantly departed
again, he looked earnestly over at Laurel.

'That's incredible! We were going to be married—
you *can't* have forgotten that, Laurel!'

Laurel was too stunned to speak for a minute or two,
but her brain was busy as she poured coffee from the
silver pot then handed his cup to him. 'Did I—marry
Diego while I was still engaged to you?' She hoped not,
because she liked the open-faced American.

He gestured impatiently with his hand. 'You sent
my ring back, said you'd fallen for this Mexican guy.'

'Diego,' she agreed softly, watching her fingers as
they moved the spoon in her cup to dissolve the sugar.
Thoughtfully, she lifted the cup to her lips, unconsciously provocative as she sipped at the strong brew.
'I'm sorry. I guess I must have fallen in love with Diego
the minute we met. He's very——'

'Rich?' Brent Halliday inserted snidely, and she
stiffened in momentary shock. What was he implying?
That she had been the kind of girl who fell for any
man providing he was well equipped with worldly
goods? Yet how was she to know that she hadn't been
a girl like that? One who had an eye to the main
chance for money and the power brought in its trail?

'He's rich, yes.'

'And he's a powerful man in Mexico. Yet he let your
father rot and *die* in one of his country's lousy jails!
What kind of a man is that? It seems to me that....'

Laurel no longer heard his indignantly raised voice.

Things were happening inside her head, roaring tumultuous things that had suddenly breached the dam of her forgetfulness and come flooding into consciousness with all the force of a tidal wave.

Her father ... Dan Trent ... a rugged, lined face whipped to a healthy tan by the ocean breezes he loved. Another Dan interposed himself as an image on her brain ... a grey-faced Dan surrounded by the drab walls of a prison. A Mexican prison, where a man was judged guilty until proven innocent ... bottles of liquor on a side table, a toast to the bride and groom ... 'May your marriage be as perfect as your mother's and mine was.' ...

The heavy iron chair scraped wildly across the terrace as she leapt to her feet and screamed '*Daddy!*' once before darkness rushed towards her. Blissful, enveloping darkness.

CHAPTER ELEVEN

LIGHT filtered dimly into the room when Laurel opened her eyes reluctantly. Juanita, sitting on a straight-backed chair beside the bed, leaned forward anxiously to scan her face, and Laurel essayed a smile intended to be reassuring. Instead, Juanita's plump features dissolved into weeping anguish.

'Oh, *señora*,' she sobbed, clutching at the slender arm nearest to her, 'I should not have let the man come in. And if I had known he would hurt you, he would have had to kill me first! *Perdon, señora.*'

Laurel summoned up a voice that seemed reluctant to leave the harsh dryness in her throat. 'It's—all right, Juanita. He didn't come to hurt me. The things he—told me brought back my memory with too much of a rush, that's all.'

Juanita's hands lifted to her face, and the eyes staring from between them were agonised. 'But Señor Diego—he will be very angry with me. He will say I should have sent the man away.'

'No, he won't. I'll—tell him that Brent gave you no choice.' Laurel's eyes narrowed on Juanita's brown orbs. 'Have you been in touch with Señor Diego?'

The housekeeper nodded vigorously. '*Si, señora.* You understand I was not able to speak with him personally, but José would give him a message at Señora Francisca Beaudry's apartment, where he was transacting business.'

Business! Like a flash from some half-forgotten

dream, a vision of Diego's head rising from Francisca's tear-stained face shot painfully across her brain. She could well imagine the type of business he was trans-acting with the sultry beauty, whose widowhood hung around her like an added attraction.

'I would like to sleep for a while now,' she lied to the agitated housekeeper, who rose reluctantly from the bedside.

'I do not like to leave you, *señora*. Señor Diego——'

'I'm going to be fine now, Juanita. I just need peace to rest for a while.'

'There is nothing I can bring for you, *señora*?'

'No, *gracias*. Just see that I'm not disturbed.'

But her thoughts went on long after the anxious housekeeper had gone from the room. Like the pieces of a scattered jigsaw puzzle, memories were falling into place. Tears welled up in her eyes when she remem-bered that Dan was dead—killed by his incarceration in a Mexican jail. Yet ... the night when they had gone to watch the divers at the El Mirador Hotel, she had noticed a tiredness about his face, and it had held the grey of illness when she had visited him in the prison. He hadn't been well then, but she had put it down first to the long haul from California to the Mexican Riviera, then the unnatural confinement in a sunless prison.

He had liked Diego, almost before he had come to know him as the provider of all human comforts apart from freedom. Freedom he had loved, with the salt spray on his face and eyes narrowed to the limitless stretch of blue before him. He had wanted her to marry Diego, sure of the Mexican's love for her in a way she herself had never been sure. Until that afternoon on the beach. . . .

Her arm came up to cover her eyes, resisting yet helpless against the moment by moment reel unfolding before her eyes. Diego's nakedness, vibrantly sensual, as he leaned over her on the beach blanket ... the warm seeking of his mouth over every hidden crevice of her body ... the feel of his passionately contoured mouth over hers, searching for and finding the response she was unable to deny.

She had loved him before that, before the sudden swamping of her senses by the purely physical appeal of him. Relentless memory, as aggressive now as it had been elusive before, ravaged her innermost being and left her weak, drained. The realisation of her love had come too late to mend a marriage born in hatred on her part. Francisca had made her untimely appearance on the scene—but Diego hadn't regarded her re-entry into his life as untimely. What could be more natural than that the embers of an old love should be fanned into flames again when he had promised an annulment to the wife he had called a shrew on several occasions? A wife his Latin pride could not accept because of his adherence to that double standard of sexual freedom for men and rigid purity for the women they married.

Until that afternoon on the beach when he had taken her and known that she had lied. . . .

Her arm lifted from her eyes suddenly and her pupils dilated as they focused sightlessly on the ceiling. *Diego had known that afternoon that her father was dead!* Why else would he have rushed down from Mexico City after receiving the phone call from the Acapulco police chief? He had made love to her with that knowledge in his mind! But why? With her father dead, the reason for their marriage was also dead. He was free to marry Francisca when the annulment went through. Had it only been lust inspired by Guillermo's youthful attack?

She bit on the knuckles of one hand. Whatever the reason, he had acted despicably, knowing as he had that Dan lay dead a few miles away.

A sudden sense of purpose sent her limbs into action, and she sprang from the bed to half-run to the walk-in closet beside the dressing table, taking down her own familiar red hide suitcase from the rack at the rear. While she stuffed clothes into its capacious interior, her mind worked as busily as her hands.

Where could she go in Acapulco without Diego finding her and bringing her back? That he would do just that she was sure of. Guilt must have generated the patient care he had lavished on her since the accident. No wonder he had been content to wait until her memory returned naturally!—maybe he had hoped it never would return in entirety. That way, he would have the best of two worlds—a submissive wife safely tucked away in Acapulco, and an ardent mistress awaiting him in Mexico City, his time neatly divided between the two.

Her mouth twisted in bitterness. He had discovered in his arrogance that she was as pure as the snow that never touched this tropical climate, so she was fit to be the mother of his children. Why go to the trouble of an annulment when he had the benefits many men would envy?

She snapped the locks on the suitcase and searched in her purse. There was sufficient money to support her for a week or so in a cheap hotel, apart from her air fare to Los Angeles. But she couldn't leave Acapulco yet. First she had to make sure where Dan had been buried. She could then make arrangements for his

transferral to the plot beside her mother's in Los
Angeles. He would have wanted that.

Was Brent still in Acapulco? As soon as the question arose in her mind she dismissed it. He was certain
to be staying in one of the plush hotels lining the beach,
and they would be the first places Diego would search.
No. She would go up into the hills beyond the Bay to
one of the cheap hotels where no questions would be
asked. She could hide out there for weeks without being
discovered.

It was only too easy to park the Jacintha Point Ford
at the airport and mingle with the newly disembarked
passengers from the Mexico City flight. Easy until she
glimpsed Diego's commanding figure in light grey
tropical suit, his hand raised imperiously to summon
a cab, which came to him immediately.

As it passed close to where she was standing she
ducked back behind a trolley laden high with suitcases,
but not before she had seen the tautly set expression on
Diego's clear-cut features. It was almost as if he had
glimpsed hell, she thought, frozen into immobility until
a porter came and wheeled away the baggage. A hell
of his own making, she reminded herself grimly as she
lined up for a taxi, her suitcase dragging at her arm.
His nicely set up world must have come tumbling down
around his ears when he had heard the news of her
sudden recovery. Had he told Francisca? He had been
with her when he received Juanita's message. As she
remembered the long weeks when he had held himself
apart from her, Laurel's mouth twisted in wry reflection. His physical needs must have been well satisfied
by the hot-blooded Mexican woman.

'*Señora?*' the taxi driver interrupted her thoughts.

'Where would you like to go?'

'Oh.' Laurel thought quickly, then indicated the road to their right leading up into the maze of narrow streets high above the glittering main avenue of Acapulco. 'A small hotel with reasonable rates,' she told him crisply, ignoring his surprised lift of dark brows. A lady of such quality, his expression clearly stated, would be more at home in one of the luxury hotels lining the Bay. Nevertheless, he drove on up the hill and finally stopped before an unprepossessing grey-white building of four stories, a hand-scrolled sign beside the entrance door proclaiming it as the Hotel Rosario.

'I will ask if they have a room for you, *señora*,' the driver turned to say. 'You wish for a single room?'

'Yes. For just a few days.'

Laurel watched his squat and far from neatly dressed figure saunter into the building and reflected sourly on the certainty that a room would be found for her at a highly inflated rate, and that the driver would casually pocket a percentage on the deal. But she was past caring about anything except the necessity for finding a hiding place from Diego. As far as that went, she eyed the depressing structure, this was the last place he would search for his runaway wife. The forlorn thought struck her then that her ploy of pretending to take a flight out of Acapulco had probably worked. Diego wouldn't be looking for her in the resort playground.

The driver emerged from the hotel and spoke through the side window. 'There is a room, *señora*,' he told her blandly, 'but it is the only one and the price is high.' He named a figure that made Laurel's mouth tighten in anger. Her suite at the Panorama had cost very little more. But she needed shelter away from

Acapulco's main thoroughfares, so she nodded tightly
and got out of the cab, waiting until the driver had
extracted her luggage from the trunk before going
into the small hotel that smelled of stale *tacos* and chili
beans. The proprietor greeted her with a bow short-
ened in deference to his ample waistline, and looked
on smirking while she signed the register under her
mother's maiden name, Olivia Forbes.

The room he showed her to was on the second floor
and primitive in the extreme. A huge ceiling fan moved
turgidly above a rickety washstand and two high-backed
chairs in sagging basketweave, while a small curtained
closet evidently served the dual purpose of wardrobe
and chest of drawers. In one corner an uncomfortable-
looking iron double bed was wedged against the wall,
its spread a dingy cream shade.

'The price is high for such a room, *señor*,' Laurel
said stiffly, her nose wrinkling in distaste.

'It is the season, *señora*,' he shrugged, his eyes bright
with speculation on her well-cut skirt suit of coffee-
coloured dacron, the smooth leather of her beige heeled
shoes. His gaze was openly curious with an underlay of
sly determination. 'You came to Acapulco without a
reservation?'

'Yes,' she admitted shortly, then added: 'But in a
few days I will be moving down closer to the beach.'

'Of course, *señora*,' he agreed smoothly. 'But now I
will bring up your luggage.'

By the time he had panted upstairs with her heavy
suitcase, Laurel had discovered that the bed creaked
alarmingly at the slightest touch, and that the overhead
fan did little more than stir the air in its immediate
vicinity, and nothing at all to relieve the clammy
humidity that made her hair cling damply to her nape

and beaded her skin with perspiration.

When she was at last alone, she stretched out on the protesting bed springs and watched the blades of the fan go slowly round. Maybe she should have tried to find Brent. She could have borrowed the money from him to cover the expense of a better room somewhere. But he would have asked questions, questions to which she had no answers. He would tell her with his lawyer's logic that Diego had no claim on her, that their marriage had been contracted out of blackmail and had no meaning now that her father was dead.

She closed her eyes to shut out the room that was in stark contrast to the opulence she had become used to at Jacintha Point. Diego might have no claim on her in a court of law, but he possessed the most important part of her ... the part that would never love again in that all-consuming way.

A distant sound of thunder penetrated the covering of sleep and Laurel started up, panicking when her eyes swept round the strange room lit only by an eerie glow from the grilled window. The hammering came again, and she slid from the creaking bed and felt her way to the door, groping for the light switch beside it.

'Who—who is it?' she quavered at the same time as she found the switch and flicked it on.

'Diego,' came the low reply, and she instinctively turned from the door, glancing round the shabby room as if seeking escape.

It was then that she saw them—tiny evil-looking creatures, scurrying across the ceiling and down the walls, fleeing to the dark crevices hidden in the plaster and woodwork.

Her ear-splitting scream brought an immediate reaction from the outside passage. There was a thump, then the sound of wood splintering as Diego kicked the door open.

'Laurel! *Querida*, what is it?'

He was beside her then, his eyes distraught as they raked her face. Wordlessly, she pointed to the disappearing scorpions and he pulled her roughly into his arms and sheltered her face against his chest.

'It is all right, *cariña*,' he soothed huskily, his hand stroking lightly over her hair. 'They will not harm you.'

He held her shuddering body until it had quietened, then put her gently from him, holding her at arm's length. She regretted the movement. She had wanted to stay pressed close to his warm chest for ever.

'Are you all right now?' At her nod, he moved his own head to indicate her unpacked suitcase. 'Is that all your luggage?'

'Yes, I—I didn't want to have to carry too much.'

His hands tightened on her shoulders as if he was about to say something, but then they dropped and he bent to pick up the suitcase.

'Come,' was all he said, and she followed him dejectedly from the room after picking up her bag and giving a cursory look around the room she hoped never to see again, trembling when she thought of the tiny creatures cavorting on the ceiling above the bed while she slept.

The proprietor met them at the bottom of the stairs and apologised ingratiatingly to Diego while casting reproachful looks in Laurel's direction.

'I am sorry, Señor Ramirez, I did not know that the Señora was your wife. She told me she was in need of a room only until her reservation became available closer to the beach.'

'And you supplied a room—at a price?' Diego queried caustically, turning with raised eyebrows to Laurel so that she told him immediately how much had been charged for the sleazy upper floor room. His eyes narrowed on the embarrassed hotel keeper.

'You will return all but one quarter of the money my wife paid you. That will be more than enough to supply a new lock for the door. Your behaviour disgraces all the respectable hotel keepers in this district.'

To the man's further obsequious apologies, Diego turned pointedly away from him after he had produced the money and ushered Laurel out into the street where the Mercedes gleamed silver at the curb. After seating her at the passenger side, he opened the rear door to thrust her suitcase in, then came to slide under the wheel. He said nothing as the sleek car slid away from the curb and headed downhill for the bright lights of Acapulco proper.

'How did you know where to find me?' Laurel asked in a low voice as they turned on to the avenue bordering the illuminated beach areas. Her eyes met the calm regard of his until he returned his attention to the road.

His tone held a shrug when he spoke. 'It wasn't too hard to work out. You had left the car at the airport, but I knew you would not have left Acapulco without ascertaining if your father was buried here or in Los Angeles. I made enquiries at the more exclusive hotels before starting on the lesser ones up on the hill, where I recognised your mother's name as the one you had given.'

Laurel's head turned sharply towards him. 'My mother's name? How could you possibly know my mother's name? I've never told you that.'

'I knew it because I stood beside her gravestone while your father was laid to rest at her side,' he said quietly, and when she drew in her breath on a painful sigh he cast her a brief sideways look. 'You remember—everything?'

'Yes.' She averted her head so that the tears shimmering in her eyes would be invisible to him. 'So they're together again. I'm glad,' she said simply, a catch in her voice. 'Thank you—for that at least.'

'At least? Why do you say that?' he was quick to ask, hardness edging his tone. 'Have I not done my best to make you happy, with pleasant surroundings and expert care, since the accident that took your memory?'

She laughed joylessly. 'I've never really believed, until now, that old saying that ignorance is bliss. And that's how you kept me, isn't it, Diego? Blissfully ignorant! You didn't even see fit to let me in on the basic fact that my father had died in your damnable jail! Oh, yes, that's bliss all right. What she doesn't know can't hurt her, including——'

'That is enough, Laurel,' he broke in sharply on her hysterically rising voice. 'We will talk at home.'

Home! Where was home for her? Not Jacintha Point, where she was Diego's name-only wife, sharing him with the woman in Mexico City who had resumed her status in his life. Not the city home of Diego Cesar Ramirez, where formal beauty abounded but no real warmth existed. The only place she had felt at home in the years since her mother's death had been Dan's boat, *Dainty*.

What had happened to *Dainty*? she wondered as Diego's foot went down on the accelerator and they sped past the impressive Aztec-styled Princess Hotel, studded with lights outlining its pyramidal shape of broad based bottom tapering to narrow top floor. It was in the penthouse of that top floor that Howard Hughes, the multi-millionaire industrialist, had spent the last hours of his life. Just as her father had spent his last hours in the glittering southernmost point of the Mexican Riviera. The only difference being, she told herself acidly, that the jail's amenities were far removed from those provided by the luxurious hotel.

The electronically controlled gates at Jacintha Point swung open to admit the car, and as it swept along the drive Laurel wondered for the first time what Juanita and Carlos had thought of her sudden disappearance. Had they known about that scene with Guillermo on the beach that fatal afternoon? She supposed they must, for she hadn't seen Guillermo since. Was it true that if Guillermo hadn't made advances to her, Diego wouldn't have either that day?

Or would he? Had he simply wanted to claim his marital rights before telling her that the reason for their marriage no longer existed? His pride ran deep, and it would be painfully scarred by the annulment of his weeks-old marriage. He hadn't known, then, that force wasn't necessary. She had loved him, so the giving of herself had been free and complete.

The bustle had gone out of Juanita's rounded figure when she came to them across the lower hall, her face wrinkled in worried lines. Her voice was subdued as she greeted them, instinctively seeking Diego's instructions regarding an evening meal.

'Whatever can be prepared within an hour,' he told her brusquely. 'We will eat in the small *sala*.'

Laurel felt drained when he left her in the master bedroom, the one she had thought never to see again. Its quiet luxury spread balm on her frayed nerves, and she was already shedding her clothes as she walked into the bathroom, envisioning a soothing massage from the jet swirl in the sunken green marble tub.

She was sitting before the wide dressing table mirror brushing through her loosened hair with long strokes when Diego came in, his skin startlingly dark against the silky white of a high-necked casual sweater. His lean hips were encased in taut off-white denim, his thick blue-black hair brushed damply back, tamed from the shower. Flames lit briefly at the back of his eyes when they flickered over the swirled green and blue of the caftan that enveloped yet emphasised all that was feminine about her.

'When you are ready, we will talk in the *sala*,' he stated calmly, belying the tense set of his shoulders. 'We have much to say to each other.'

'Have we?' she countered, gazing intently into the mirror as she clipped two huge turquoise-coloured rings to her ears before standing up. 'I'd have thought it was pretty clear cut. My father is dead, so there is no longer any reason for our marriage.'

Anger struggled with control in his mobile features, and at last he said flatly: 'Our marriage is a fact, *querida*. We cannot alter that now.'

She moved restlessly away and moved aside the delicate lace curtains covering the full-length windows. The moon, still not risen high in the sky, sent a silver arrow across the ocean and bathed the outer scene with an eerie radiance.

'There's such a thing as a special dispensation,' she shrugged, unprepared for his noiseless progress over the thick carpet on the fierce jab of his fingers as he spun her round to face him.

'Why?' he rasped savagely. 'Why do you torture me

so, when we could be happy together?' His fingers
raked painfully through her hair, dragging her face up
to the demand in his. Hoarsely, he questioned: 'Were
we not happy that day on the beach, *querida*? You
wanted me as much as I wanted you. Admit it, Laurel,
admit it!'

She stared half scared into the animal glare in his
eyes, then her lids fell to obscure the answering leap
in the darkened green of her eyes. How could she deny
remembrance of that afternoon when passion had leapt
between them, urged on by the restless rise and fall of
the ocean behind them?

'You know it is so,' he muttered hotly, and pulled
her face to a position just under his own, his mouth
coming down hard suddenly on hers, brushing abrasively over her lips until they parted with a sigh of
resignation.

Her senses drowned in the sheer physical impact of
him, her palms stroking the smooth muscled chest
under the silk fibres of his sweater. How experienced
he was!—and not only with her. There must have been
so many women in his life, not least of whom was Francisca.... Did he kiss her this way at their meetings in
Mexico City? Lift her yielding body in strong arms and
carry her lightly to the bed, nuzzling his lips at that
vulnerable spot beneath her ear and——

She pushed against his chest with all her strength
and the suddenness of her attack slackened his possessive hold on her. In another second she had rolled to
the far side of the bed and bounced to her feet, shaking
as she turned to rake him contemptuously with her
eyes.

'Don't you dare touch me ever again! Save your

Latin lover act for Francisca, I'm sure she appreciates
it!'

Her brain refused the assessment of her eyes, which
told her that Diego was genuinely bewildered by her
accusation. Shaking his head, he got slowly to his feet
and stepped round the bed to meet her.

'I don't understand. What has Francisca to do with
you and me?'

Laurel laughed, her voice brittle. 'She has nothing
to do with me. With you? Plenty! Have you forgotten,
Diego? I remember it all clearly now, everything that
happened, from your spending the night with Francisca after I'd found you kissing her, to the time you
made love to me on the beach knowing my father was
lying dead a few miles away! You're the most despic-
able man I've——'

'No! That is not true!' He caught her by the wrist
and swung her round to face him again. The glow had
leached from under his tan, leaving his skin a faint
yellow colour. 'I admit that I forced myself on you that
day at the beach, but——' he shook his head again, his
eyes bleakly sincere, 'I swear to you I had no knowledge
of your father's death that afternoon.'

'You must have!' she cried, pulling free and going
to sink with trembling legs on the dressing table stool.
'The police chief called me here on the day you saw
the Justice Minister. When he said that my father had
—gone, I thought he meant that—that. . . .' She drew a
deep breath. 'I thought he meant that Dad had been
moved closer to Mexico City, and that he wanted to let
you know that he'd set things going for an early trial.
I—I gave him numbers where he could reach you in
Mexico City.'

Diego moved to stand behind her, his hands searing her shoulder skin with their dry warmth. 'I received no call from the Acapulco police chief. I was already on my way down here to tell you that the Justice Minister had been in touch with me to tell me that the two men who chartered your father's boat had been found, and that they had cleared him completely of any complicity in their scheme to export drugs from Mexico.'

Feeling as if the tendons on her neck might snap, Laurel raised her eyes to meet his in the wide mirror above the dressing table.

'You mean,' she whispered, 'that—Dad would have been free anyway?'

'Yes,' he said simply. 'It was only later, after the accident to your head, that I knew of his death.' His hands slid tenatively over her back. 'How could you have believed that I made love to you knowing that my good friend Dan lay dead not far away?' he asked emotionally.

'I—I thought you wanted the best of two worlds,' she admitted wanly. 'Francisca in Mexico City, and me here. That you wanted to—make sure of me before I found out about my father.'

'*Cristo!*' he swore softly, and moved away from her, lifting one hand to rub angrily the taut tendons at the back of his neck, then made a confession she had never thought to hear from him. 'I will never understand the working of a woman's mind if I live for a thousand years! Could you not tell that I loved you too much to be denied that day on the beach? How could I love you that way if I had another woman in Mexico City? I am no gigolo, like Guillermo, to pretend love with a woman. It is you I loved, from the instant I saw you. How could you think that Francisca or any other woman could ever compare with you in my heart?'

'It wasn't hard!' Laurel retorted hotly. 'Didn't I see you kiss her with my own eyes, and—and later know that you had spent the night with her?'

'You were jealous, *niña*?' Far from being dismayed at her accusation, he seemed delighted.

'Yes, damn you, I was jealous! It was that night that I—I knew that I loved you, and I waited for you to come as you'd promised, then I—I saw you leave with Francisca and knew you'd forgotten all about me.'

'Oh, *querida*!' Two steps brought him back to her, his arms reaching down to bring her to her feet and enfold her within their circle. 'I spent part of that night with Francisca, true. And I had just kissed her cheek when you came into the study with your demands that I do something immediately for your father.' His hand slid down to hers and he led her to the bed. 'Come here, *cariña*, and let me explain about Francisca.' When they were seated side by side on the bed, his warm hand at her waist conveying his feeling as much as his huskily emotional voice did, he went on:

'When we were very young, Francisca and I were betrothed to each other. We were children at the time, but our respective parents thought it would be a good match. As it would have been,' his eyes twinkled suddenly into hers, 'if Anton had not come into her life, and if I had not had a dream of the girl who would one day be my wife.' He sighed.

'Then Anton died, and Francisca returned to Mexico. Anton's business affairs were in a bad state, and Francisca asked my help in sorting them out. That night when you saw her in my arms was as innocent as if I had held my grandmother to comfort her. I went to Francisca's apartment with her, but stayed only a short time. The rest of the night I spent trying not to come to you.'

'Not——?'

'If I had come, *querida*, I would have made you my wife that night,' he declared solemnly, though there was a mocking gleam far back in his eyes. 'And you hated me for forcing you into marriage with me in order to help your father. How could I risk it?'

Laurel straightened away from him to stare into the dark depths of his eyes where yellow motes danced. 'But you really didn't want a wife you thought was—impure, did you? You walked out on me on our wedding night because you thought I had been with Brent before you.'

Diego shook his head negatively. 'I did not leave you because of the possibility that you had been with an-other man. Though I will not pretend that the thought hurt my—what do you call it?—Latin temperament. No, it was because you called his name at a time when mine should have been on your lips, if you loved me. For the same reason I promised you freedom from our marriage when your father was released from prison. And then——'

'Then?' she prompted when he paused, and he smiled slightly down into her eyes.

'Then when your memory was gone you told me that you loved me, that you wanted me as much as I desired you.' She felt the taut stiffening of his backbone. 'But how could I take you when you knew nothing of what had gone before? When I had forced you to——?'

Laurel laid her fingers over his lips. 'If memory serves me now, I don't recall you having to use too much force that day on the beach.' She lifted a hand to stroke the thick hair at his temple. 'Are you telling me that you've really loved me all along?'

'More than the moon loves the stars, or the sea loves the rocks it comes back to time after time,' he said solemnly with a romantic overtone that brought tingles to her spine. But there was one more problem teasing at the back of her mind.

'Even if I don't come up to your mother's high standards?' she said half teasingly, swaying towards him but pulling back when a frown sliced down between his eyes.

'My mother? What does she have to do with us?'

Awkwardly, Laurel said: 'It's just that—well, Consuelo seems to think that you have a mother fixation, and that you—married me because I resemble her.'

Diego smiled bitterly. 'If I had a mother fixation, it would only be to remind me of which wife I should *not* choose.' Looking down into Laurel's shocked eyes, he went on brusquely: 'My mother was what the psychiatrists call a nymphomaniac. She could never have her fill of men—young men, old ones, married ones, single ones. My father was bringing her back from her married lover when they were killed in the plane crash.'

'Oh, Diego, I'm sorry,' she breathed, covering his hand in an instinctive gesture of comfort. 'I didn't know.'

His shoulders lifted in a shrug. 'Not many people do, apart from my grandmother. She hated my mother for what she did to my father.'

'I don't blame her,' Laurel shuddered, accepting the arm he slid round her and feeling the smooth silk of his sweater beneath her cheek. 'Diego?' she said tremulously.

'Yes?'

'Could we start again, do you think? I mean——'

'Where would you suggest we start, *mi esposa*?' he

interrupted in a deep tone, his hand running familiarly over the sharply outlined contours of her body, making her insides feel like candle wax melting under a flame. 'Here?'

'Everywhere,' she commanded huskily, and forgot everything in her pleasure at being wooed by Diego in his expert way until a shocked Spanish voice said from the doorway:

'*Señor! Señora! Perdon!* The meal is ready.'

Diego's head lifted from Laurel's and he stared in abstracted amusement at the embarrassed housekeeper. 'Keep it warm,' he instructed drily, and returned his attention to Laurel's parted lips. 'As we are keeping our marriage warm,' he muttered under his breath, and Laurel smiled at him from the bed pillows with sudden happiness.

'Let's raise the temperature to hot,' she murmured provocatively against his lips.

Mills & Boon Classics

The very best of Mills & Boon
romances, brought back for those of
you who missed reading them
when they were first published.

In

June

we bring back the following four
great romantic titles.

ONE MAN'S HEART
by *Mary Burchell*

A harmless — well, fairly harmless — escapade took an
unexpected and horrifying turn that nearly landed Hilma in
serious trouble. But fortunately there was a handsome and
chivalrous stranger at hand to help her.

THE KISSES AND THE WINE
by *Violet Winspear*

Lise supposed she ought to be grateful to the imperious Conde
Leandro de Marcos Reyes for helping her out of an awkward
situation — but not so grateful that she was willing to repay
him as he suggested, by pretending to be his fiancée. A
domineering Spanish nobleman was not her idea of a comfortable husband. However, she reluctantly agreed to the
deception, just for a short time . . .

THE WATERFALLS OF THE MOON
by *Anne Mather*

'He's allergic to emotional entanglements,' Ruth declared after
she encountered the disturbing Patrick Hardy. But it was an
allergy that Ruth unfortunately didn't share and she tricked
Patrick into marriage and accompanied him to Venezuela.
Would her husband ever forgive the deception?

MAN IN CHARGE
by *Lilian Peake*

Juliet was delighted to get the job at Majors boutique, and full
of ideas and enthusiasm about it — but she found herself
continually in conflict with the man in charge, the chairman's
son, Drew Major. She wanted to keep the job — but was it
worth it, if it meant fighting this cynical man every step of
the way?

The Mills & Boon Rose is the Rose of Romance

Every month there are ten new titles to choose from — ten new stories about people falling in love, people you want to read about, people in exciting, far-away places. Choose Mills & Boon. It's your way of relaxing.

June's titles are:

JACINTHA POINT by *Elizabeth Graham*
To save her father, Laurel had been forced to marry the masterful Diego Ramirez, a man she did not know and certainly did not love.

FUGITIVE WIFE by *Sara Craven*
Briony had no doubts about her love for Logan Adair. Yet their marriage had been nothing but a farce from the very beginning.

A FROZEN FIRE by *Charlotte Lamb*
What would happen to Helen's sense of duty to her blatantly unfaithful husband now that Mark Eliot had come into her life?

TRADER'S CAY by *Rebecca Stratton*
There was bound to be tension between Francesca and Antonio Morales, but it was Francesca's relationship with his son Andrés that caused the real trouble between the two of them . . .

KISS OF A TYRANT by *Margaret Pargeter*
When Stacy Weldon first met Sloan Maddison he seemed decidedly antagonistic to her; yet why should he concern himself over the job his mother had offered her?

THE LAIRD OF LOCHARRUN by *Anne Hampson*
What had the formidable Craig Lamond been told about Lorna to make him so hostile to her?

NO WAY OUT by *Jane Donnelly*
Lucy's beloved twin sister had pretended to Daniel Stewart that she was in fact Lucy, and it shouldn't have been difficult for Lucy to deceive him in her turn. But . . .

THE ARRANGED MARRIAGE by *Flora Kidd*
Roselle's marriage to Léon Chauvigny had never been a real one. Now the time had come to end it once and for all. Or had it?

OUTBACK RUNAWAY by *Dorothy Cork*
Running away from the heartbreak of a disastrous love affair, all Dale found was Trelawney Saber, with a bracingly unsympathetic attitude to her troubles!

VALLEY OF THE HAWK by *Margaret Mayo*
Damon Courtney jumped to all the wrong conclusions about Corrie — and turned her life upside down in the process!

If you have difficulty in obtaining any of these books from your local paperback retailer, write to:

Mills & Boon Reader Service
P.O. Box 236, Thornton Road, Croydon, Surrey, CR9 3RU.

The Mills & Boon Rose is the Rose of Romance

Look for the Mills & Boon Rose next month

CHANCE MEETING *by Kay Thorpe*
Lee Brent was socially and financially right out of Sharon's
league, and the last thing she wanted was to discover why he
had really married her . . .

PRISONER IN PARADISE *by Marjorie Lewty*
Stranded in Mexico, Sara's rescuer was the formidable Jason
Knight, who made no secret of his low opinion of her.

SET THE STARS ON FIRE *by Sally Wentworth*
When actress Lori West joined a film company in Rhodes, she
was aware of hostility from everyone there — in particular
from the director, Lewis Brent.

HALF A WORLD AWAY *by Gloria Bevan*
On a trip to New Zealand, Nicola met and fell in love with
Keith Lorimer, but he didn't seem to feel anything but
friendship for her . . .

YESTERDAY'S SCARS *by Carole Mortimer*
Because of what had once passed between Hazel and her stern
cousin-guardian Rafe Savage, she found he was now bitter and
unforgiving, scarred in more than body . . .

CAROLINE'S WATERLOO *by Betty Neels*
Could Caroline settle for a marriage to the imposing Professor
Radinck Thoe van Erckelens when it was clear that there was
to be no romance involved?

THE LEO MAN *by Rebecca Stratton*
James Fraser was a typical Leo man, thought Rowan — bossy!
But she found herself rapidly revising her opinion.

A RING FOR A FORTUNE *by Lilian Peake*
Sloan Lancaster agreed to marry Jasmine so that she could
inherit her grandfather's fortune, although Sloan made no
pretence of feeling anything for her but contempt . . .

MISS HIGH AND MIGHTY *by Margaret Rome*
How could Jade convince her husband, the lordly Dom Diego
da Luz Pereira da Silves, that he was wrong to accuse her of
marrying him for his money?

THE BUTTERFLY AND THE BARON *by Margaret Way*
Renee Dalton was a rich society butterfly, and the forceful,
down-to-earth Nick Garbutt had no opinion of her at all.

If you have difficulty in obtaining any of these books from
your local paperback retailer, write to:

Mills & Boon Reader Service
P.O. Box 236, Thornton Road, Croydon, Surrey, CR9 3RU.

Available July 1980